Please Evacuate

A gay, partygoing New Yorker unconcerned about the future or the unsustainability of capitalism is hit by a truck and thrust into a straight man's body half a continent away. As Hunter tries to figure out what's happening, he's caught up in another disaster, a wildfire sweeping through a Colorado community, the flames overtaking him and several schoolchildren as they flee.

When he awakens, Hunter finds himself in the body of yet another man, this time in northern Italy, a former missionary about to marry a young Mormon woman. Still piecing together this new reality, and beginning to embrace his latest identity, Hunter fights for his life in a devastating flash flood along with his wife *and* his new husband.

He's an aging worker in drought-stricken Texas, a nurse at an assisted living facility in the direct path of a hurricane, an advocate for the unhoused during a freak Seattle blizzard.

We watch as Hunter is plunged into life after life, finally recognizing the futility of only looking out for #1 and understanding the part he must play in addressing the global climate crisis…if he ever gets another chance.

Praise for Johnny Townsend

In *Zombies for Jesus*, "Townsend isn't writing satire, but deeply emotional and revealing portraits of people who are, with a few exceptions, quite lovable."

Kel Munger, *Sacramento News and Review*

In *Sex among the Saints,* "Townsend writes with a deadpan wit and a supple, realistic prose that's full of psychological empathy....he takes his protagonists' moral struggles seriously and invests them with real emotional resonance."

Kirkus Reviews

Let the Faggots Burn: The UpStairs Lounge Fire is "a gripping account of all the horrors that transpired that night, as well as a respectful remembrance of the victims."

Terry Firma, Patheos

"Johnny Townsend's 'Partying with St. Roch' [in the anthology *Latter-Gay Saints*] tells a beautiful, haunting tale."

Kent Brintnall, Out in Print: Queer Book Reviews

Selling the City of Enoch is "sharply intelligent...pleasingly complex...The stories are full of...doubters, but there's no vindictiveness in these pages; the characters continuously poke holes in Mormonism's more extravagant absurdities, but they take very little pleasure in doing so....Many of Townsend's stories...have a provocative edge to them, but this [book] displays a great deal of insight as well...a playful, biting and surprisingly warm collection."

Kirkus Reviews

Gayrabian Nights is "an allegorical tour de force...a hard-core emotional punch."

Gay. Guy. Reading and Friends

The Washing of Brains has "A lovely writing style, and each story [is] full of unique, engaging characters....immensely entertaining."

Rainbow Awards

In *Dead Mankind Walking*, "Townsend writes in an energetic prose that balances crankiness and humor....A rambunctious volume of short, well-crafted essays..."

Kirkus Reviews

Please Evacuate

Johnny Townsend

Copyright © 2022 Johnny Townsend

Print ISBN: 979-8-9878666-6-5
Ebook ISBN: 979-8-9878666-7-2

Printed on acid-free paper.

2023

Second Edition

Cover design by BetiBup33 Studio Design

Special thanks to Donna Banta

for her editorial assistance

For more of Donna's own work,

please read *Mormon Erotica* and *Seer Stone*.

Contents

Section One: Swept Away

I awoke from a nightmare in which I was drowning and found myself lying next to a naked woman. In the dim light, I could just make out the olive coloring of her skin and her thick, dark hair. The woman's nipples pointed toward the ceiling.

I screamed.

"What!?" The woman beside me sat up with her hand on her bare breasts. I'd never done drag, so I couldn't begin to guess their official size. But they were decidedly large. "What's wrong, honey?"

"Who are you?" I demanded. My eyes darted quickly about the room, the possibility that my dad was somehow behind this flashing insanely through my brain. I could just make out photos in large plastic frames on top of a dresser and a painting of a cow on the far wall. Not a gay man's bedroom.

What kind of folks *did* hang paintings of cows in their bedroom?

"Where am I?"

"Oh, honey!" The woman reached over to caress the side of my head. She had well-manicured nails, belying her taste in room décor, and her eyebrows were carefully plucked, suggesting a missing isthmus.

Was she trans? A sheet covered potentially useful information.

"Who are you?" I repeated.

"Are you serious?" Her eyes narrowed. "Do we need to get you to the hospital?"

I pulled away from the woman. The nightlight gave off enough of a glow to reveal the worry in her eyes, more suspicious than genuine.

But I'd never gone home with a woman before. Still a virgin at thirty-five as far as that was concerned.

Men, though, I'd awakened beside plenty of times over the past fifteen years. Never enough men, of course, but there were decades left to improve that tally.

The woman reached for me again and this time touched the back of my head. It hurt.

If this was PTSD, it was late in coming. I'd refused grief counseling after Dad's death.

"You think you have a concussion?" she asked. When I frowned, she returned the look. "You fell and hit your head," she explained, enunciating carefully, "when we were stepping out of the shower last night."

"I did?" I asked. "We…we showered together?" Had someone slipped me some LSD?

"Nick, you better not be jerking me around." The woman's lips tightened. I wondered if they'd been around my cock earlier. I wondered— "You promised to watch Jamie in the morning so I could do the building inspection."

"My name's not Nick."

The woman rolled her eyes. "For God's sake, are you role-playing again?" She stole a glance at the clock on the bedside table. "It's frickin' 3:00 in the morning."

"My name's Hunter," I said firmly.

"You sure it's not Peter? 'Cause you're being a dick. You know I don't like sex in the middle of the night."

"I don't want sex, either," I told her. I lifted the sheet to see that I was nude, too. How in the world was I going to get out of here?

Wherever here was.

"I want to go home."

At this, the woman's frown finally disappeared, replaced by a soft smile. "Little boy lost?" she suggested.

"I'm not little."

The woman reached for me under the sheet. "You are now but I can change that."

"Who are you?"

The woman's smile widened slightly. "Amnesia, huh? We haven't tried that one yet." She pulled the sheet up over her like a cape and straddled me. "Let me see if I can spark some memories."

Oh, I had memories. Dad giving me monthly testosterone injections starting on my thirteenth birthday. Him groaning every time he'd been forced to introduce me to a friend or acquaintance. "We should never have named you Hunter," he'd tell me afterward. "But no one wants to name their son Florist or Figure Skater."

For someone who didn't like sex in the middle of the night, the naked woman on top of me put in a valiant effort. Given my terror, confusion, and thorough lack of interest, it took a good three minutes before I grew hard and another five before I came.

Afterward, she rolled over and went to sleep. I did, too. Figured this was all a dream, anyway—at least a wet nightmare—and when I woke up later, I'd actually wake up.

I didn't.

I still seemed to be Nick and still didn't know this woman's name, afraid to ask since she'd written off my confusion earlier as a joke. I could hardly start guessing like Jerry Seinfeld had in an old rerun I'd once watched.

"Mulva?"

What if I used to be straight, I wondered, until I bumped my head? What if it was the *other* life I seemed to remember that was the dream? All those visions of dicks…maybe I was a urologist.

And what if the opposite had happened? I didn't think I'd ever been into S&M, but what if I used to be gay and some injury had turned me straight?

Mom had always said she hoped Dad could beat the gay away. I hadn't been charged when I pushed him in front of a gas truck during the last beating he ever gave me. We were on a father-son outing, planning to "rough it" in the woods, but we never reached the state park. When we stopped at a gas station to refuel, he caught me ogling the cashier.

Yikes.

What if *he'd* jumped into another life after I'd killed him and was now beating someone else's kid?

The woman beside me moaned as she slowly awakened. "Can you make sure the kids are up?" she mumbled.

"Sure…sweetie."

"Even Jamie. I know she's sick, but she needs to eat."

First, I headed to the bathroom, en suite so easy to find. I peed before daring to look in the mirror.

That definitely wasn't me. Just urinating a moment earlier had proven that, of course. The head of Nick's dick was larger than mine. Not quite a toadstool, but the instrument would be challenging for some guys to take.

Nick's nose was smaller than my own, almost narrow, his stubble so slight he probably only needed to shave every other day. His hair was straight and sandy, his ears flatter against the side of his head. Nice hair pattern on his chest.

Not bad, I thought, in a dad bod kind of way.

I caressed my right nipple and watched as my penis twitched.

Damn, I kind of wanted to have sex with that guy in the mirror.

Not the first time I realized I was a narcissist.

I slipped through the bedroom, the woman sitting groggily on the edge of the bed, and entered the hallway. Before anyone could catch my ignorance, I started opening doors and peeking inside.

"Rise and shine!"

Three kids. All I could find, at least.

I reached the kitchen first, wondering if I should scramble some eggs. But there weren't any in the fridge. I opened a cabinet and found four types of breakfast cereal. I set them all on the table, along with a stack of bowls and a jug of milk. Anticipating the needs of others wasn't really my forte, but I needed to deflect attention until I could figure out what was going on.

Alien experimentation?

Sometimes, dreams felt real until you woke up, and then you realized instantly how impossible they'd been. I didn't remember ever having a dream this vivid before, but then, who remembered dreams for more than a few minutes? It was impossible to know if they felt this real in the moment.

But I'd learned years ago how to take an active role in my dreams. If I didn't like the way the story was playing out, I would "rewind" the scene and do something different. That all seemed perfectly logical in the dream itself.

So I was a husband and dad for now. But if I was staying home from work today to take care of my sick daughter, perhaps I could give her some alcohol-based cold medicine and tell her to take a nap after everyone else left while I called a plumber or kept an eye out for the mail carrier for some extramarital play.

No point letting a dream go to waste.

As I poured myself some oatmeal crunch, I listened to the sound of the shower in the en suite and light footsteps in the hallway shuffling down to another bathroom. I started chomping on my cereal while trying to reconstruct the events of the previous evening.

Food had never tasted this real in a dream before.

Had it?

I took another bite and chomped some more. Perhaps someone had slipped Rohypnol into my drink last night and this was all a big practical joke. Or revenge for sleeping with someone's husband. A mad scientist's bizarre research project.

I couldn't finish the cereal.

Where were the damn kids?

I licked my spoon dry and struck my head with it several times. Was that a B flat? "Wake up!" I ordered myself out loud.

The last thing I remembered before finding myself in bed with a woman was strutting into a Lamborghini dealership to impress…what was his name?

Jonathan. An attorney I'd met at a professionals bar in Manhattan. We'd gone out a time or two, he had a big dick and a gifted tongue, and I wanted to prove my competitive worth despite my smaller dick.

Slightly smaller.

"You live in Chelsea and you want to buy a gas guzzler like that?"

I wasn't sure what kind of law Jonathan specialized in. When he started talking about environmental justice, my eyes glazed over.

"We could zip up to the Hamptons," I said. "Or spend a weekend in Montreal."

"We could take a train," he countered, "or rent a more reasonable car."

The conversation had deteriorated quickly after that. Jonathan began acting all holier-than-thou and I decided I could find a guy with an even bigger dick and more gifted tongue if I started cruising around in a Lamborghini. I'd just been promoted, after all, my new office providing a great view of the Hudson. No reason not to live life to the fullest.

It was time to trade in my Jag anyway.

The last thing I remembered was giving Jonathan the finger as I pulled onto 11th, leaving him to find his own way home.

No.

The last thing I remembered was hearing a horn blaring in my ear and turning to see a tanker truck bearing down on the passenger side of the car.

A girl wandered into the kitchen wearing pajamas covered with yellow butterflies. She looked to be about six. Or four. Maybe seven.

"Morning, pumpkin."

She frowned and sat at the far end of the table, pouring herself some cereal and milk.

Probably not four.

Only a moment later, two other kids stumbled into the kitchen, a boy about ten and another girl, maybe eight?

"Hey." I nodded a greeting.

I had a wife and three kids. God was real and I was in hell.

The boy and the older girl started fighting over one of the cereal boxes. "Stop it, Juniper!" the boy called out.

"You stop, Jaren! You finished the box last time."

"Juniper!"

Eternal damnation. Of all things for my dad to be right about.

"Jaren!"

"Oh. My. God," I said, and something in my tone made the kids stop and turn toward me. "Did your parents really name you that?"

Juniper pursed her lips just as her mother had a few hours earlier, and the two older children exchanged a look. The younger girl, Jamie, I supposed, seemed oblivious, fishing for one of the multi-colored globs floating in her bowl.

"Mrs. Howell said we should turn our parents in if they use drugs," Jaren announced, apropos of nothing.

"Mrs. Howell probably needs to get laid," I told him.

All three kids stared at me, though they were too young to understand what I'd said. My subconscious was making them more sophisticated than real kids.

But this all *felt* real. What if some metaphysical something-or-other had done this? No one in their right mind would believe me. I'd be locked up and put in a straitjacket.

I was Jennifer Love Hewitt explaining to someone in every episode of *Ghost Whisperer* why they needed to believe the unbelievable.

Only the person I needed to convince of the truth was *me*.

My heart began beating faster and a drop of sweat trickled down my left temple. I heard footsteps approaching and wondered how I was going to keep up this charade. Perhaps it didn't matter if the woman called someone to cart me off to an institution. I was clearly delusional.

But first, goddammit, I was going to have a meal with my family.

I'd always eaten breakfast alone growing up, even when my parents were at the table. They'd have bacon and eggs, maybe some buttered toast, while I was handed an off-brand Pop-Tart. It wasn't that Mom was negligent. She genuinely believed I preferred the dry pastry.

I think.

Dinner, though, that was different. Mom always prepared enough of the good stuff—roast beef with carrots and potatoes, steak and corn on the cob—while also preparing punishment food, usually a can of potted meat, just for me in case she or Dad caught me doing something unmanly before dinner.

Like reading a book. Or listening to the Backstreet Boys.

"Good morning!" my wife said in a faux cheerful tone as she walked into the kitchen. Her half-closed eyelids suggested the shower hadn't been as successful as she'd hoped, but she was still alert enough to see that Jaren and Juniper were both clutching the same box.

"If there's not enough," the woman said, "just mix in some other cereal. It'll make a new flavor. Be adventurous. It's the only way to get ahead in life."

Jaren groaned and released his hold on the box. Juniper ripped it away victoriously and poured the last of the contents into her bowl, so much there was hardly any room left for milk.

The woman began asking the kids what their upcoming day at school looked like, and I retreated from the conversation. I could hardly start calling her "Mother" like a dad in a 1950s sit-com. Perhaps when everyone was gone, I'd have a chance to find some addressed mail, a passport maybe. Look up the news online to see what day it was. Call someone.

Not Jonathan.

Jamie sneezed, spraying the table with milk.

"Gross!" Jaren shouted.

"You're such a baby," Juniper told her sister.

"Be nice," the woman said, grabbing a paper towel from the counter and wiping Jamie's face and then the table. "She's sick. Your dad'll be staying home to watch her."

Damn. How long was this dream going to last?

I knew it wasn't a dream.

Or it was and it wasn't, like Captain Picard's experience in "The Inner Light," when he witnesses the last days of a world whose sun is dying.

Jamie didn't even seem all that sick. Probably just trying to get out of school.

Or kindergarten. I still didn't know how old she was.

Even if I hadn't been gay, I wouldn't have had any kids. No way I was wasting my youth and my money and my (natural!) testosterone worrying about someone else's future. I had my own now to concentrate on—Halloween in San Francisco, Mardi Gras in Sydney, Southern Decadence in New Orleans.

"Won't you, Nick?" I heard someone say and slowly began noticing again the other people at the table.

I looked at the woman sitting across from me.

"Won't you?" she repeated.

"Um…"

"You will look up some more memory exercises we can try tonight?" she asked.

"Absolutely," I said.

The woman smiled and gave me a wink.

Perhaps this was only Purgatory.

Soon, breakfast was over, the woman was out the door on her way to work, and I still didn't know her name. Jaren and Jupiter followed soon after, heading to the corner where the school bus would pick them up. We were apparently in suburbia.

Hell. Definitely hell.

I was about to turn on the TV when Jamie held up a hand. "Mom'll be mad if you don't put the dishes in the dishwasher."

Surely, whatever this was couldn't drag through the whole day, but just in case, I did as Jamie directed while she sat at the table and observed. She didn't cough or sneeze once.

"Are you really sick?" I asked. "Or was someone mean to you at school?"

Uh-oh. I forgot I didn't know if she was even in school yet.

The girl remained silent, and I was afraid I'd been caught.

"Jamie?"

"Mrs. Forster keeps making me stand in the corner with my nose against the wall."

"Excuse me?" I stopped and turned to look at her. What *year* was this, anyway? The kitchen appliances looked reasonably contemporary. "Whatever for?"

Jamie shrugged. "I don't think she likes when people have more than two kids."

My mouth fell open.

"I'll have a talk with Mrs. Forster," I said.

I wouldn't really. I wouldn't be here that long. But the promise needed to be made.

Then again, what did I care about this girl I didn't even know? I closed my eyes.

It wasn't *fair* for adults to ruin a child's life.

"What would you like to do today, pumpkin?"

We watched a couple of movies. *Encanto* and *Up*. When Jamie fell asleep on the sofa next to me, I brushed the hair off her forehead and realized she did feel warm. Maybe she *was* sick.

I turned the volume down on the TV and switched to cable to watch some news and get my bearings. The local channels seemed to be centered in Denver.

I'd never bothered to visit this town before.

The Antarctic was 70 degrees warmer than usual for this time of year, the Arctic 60 degrees warmer. A car bomb had exploded in Afghanistan. Lawmakers in Idaho were trying to put parents of trans kids in prison. Oil prices in the U.S. were lower this week but gas prices were higher. Thirteen people had drowned in a subway in China.

My head hurt. I touched the back of my head and winced.

Everyone had seen enough science fiction shows to "believe" weird crap was possible. *Stranger Things, Quantum Leap, Dr. Who*. No one believed a fairy tale like "Jack and the Beanstalk," but some of these other scenarios we kept in the part of our brain reserved for "Not really but maybe. Who knows? Why not? No way."

Perhaps I'd ruptured a blood vessel in that part of my brain and damaged it.

A loud honking screech blared out of the television in repeated bursts. Jamie stirred beside me and slowly sat up. A newscaster appeared off to one side of the screen while the other two thirds showed an aerial view of a massive wildfire sweeping toward a street lined with new construction. A few of the buildings looked freshly completed, with new sod in rectangles and signs posted near the sidewalk. Smoke billowed high into the air.

Three tiny figures ran out of one of the finished houses, the camera zooming in while one of the figures jumped into a car. Jamie stiffened beside me.

"That's Mom!" she shouted.

I honestly couldn't recognize the figure in all the commotion, and I hadn't watched this morning to see what she was driving. Jamie was probably just assuming the worst. It certainly didn't look good for whoever those people were. Some of the new construction was now burning, the flames jumping and spreading fast. Smoke crossed the road in both directions. We watched as the woman took off and disappeared into the blackness. The roof of the house she'd exited only moments before caught fire.

"Officials have issued an evacuation order for residents on the west side of Superior. The wildfire is heading toward the McCaslin Boulevard/Coalton Road area."

"Is that anywhere near us, pumpkin?" I asked quietly.

Jamie looked up at me and shrugged, turning back to stare at the images on the television. I stood and nonchalantly headed to the kitchen for a glass of water, really searching for a cell phone. Jamie's mother would have hers with her, so anything left here would be Nick's.

Yep, there it was, recharging on the counter. I picked it up and turned it on.

Locked.

But it used facial recognition, thank God, and not a pin.

I casually looked out the front window to read the address on the house across the street.

"What street do we live on, pumpkin?" No way to ask that without sounding like an idiot, but I could see smoke from here. It didn't look far away.

This was a suburb, for God's sake, not some rural mining town in the mountains. Folks from the three houses I could see through our front window were throwing a few things into their cars and taking off.

I scrolled through Nick's contacts but didn't know which of the female names was his wife's.

Why wasn't *she* calling?

"They're evacuating the schools!" Jamie squealed from the sofa. "Daddy! What's going to happen to Juniper and Jaren?"

What kind of hell had I found myself in?

"What's the name of your school?" I asked. All three kids must still attend the same one.

"John Moore." She stood in front of the television, leaning forward and staring.

I couldn't find a school with that name but tried "Jon" instead. Nothing. Then "John M." And suddenly "John Muir" popped up. "You know how to get there from here, pumpkin?"

Jamie shook her head. I'd use GPS.

"Get dressed," I said quietly. "We're going to get your brother and sister." I tried to figure out where Nick might keep his keys and found them next to his wallet in a little nook near the entrance to the laundry room.

There were shouts outside, the sound of tires squealing. By the time we pulled onto the street, traffic was thick but moving.

Too bad this guy didn't have a faster car. It didn't *have* to be a Lamborghini. An Alfa Romeo would do.

"In 500 feet, turn left," a voice on Nick's phone told me. Almost half the sky was black, and the voice was leading me toward the worst of it.

Would it be wrong to just drive away? Even if this was all a bad dream, I'd heard that if you died in your dream, you really did die. Of course, how could there ever have been a study to prove that?

It took almost ten minutes on the increasingly clogged roads to approach the school. Two dozen cars were lined up in front, with parents standing beside open doors and waving at the crowds streaming from the building. A few buses were in the school bus driveway and teachers and staff were running toward their cars in the parking lot.

Several of the teachers ushered small children to hurry along with them. Two middle-aged women wearing orange vests over their regular clothing pushed kids into buses. A handful of parents found their kids and floored their gas pedals getting away.

It was a miracle no one was run over.

There was no such thing as miracles.

"Jaren!" Jamie called out her window. "Juniper!" No one could possibly hear in the midst of all the shouting and yelling and crackling and creaking and groaning. The wind had picked up and roared all around us. Hot embers flew high overhead.

Could I even remember what the kids looked like? I'd only seen them a few minutes this morning.

I looked over my shoulder and saw several homes burning a block back. Up ahead, a single home was ablaze.

The roof of the gymnasium caught fire. Parents honked their horns and screamed.

"Makisha!"

"Terry!"

"Christopher!"

"Baran!"

Every year, I heard about things like this. Paradise going up in flames. Lytton. Pine City. Gatlinburg. All places no one important lived. And those people knew what risks they were taking when they moved there. Like the idiots who lived in basement apartments that got flooded. Like the morons who lived in avalanche country.

I stepped out of my car. "Just grab a kid and go!" I shouted. But parents wouldn't leave without their own.

What, after all, did I understand about family ties? I didn't even send my mom Christmas cards.

She didn't send me any, either.

I needed to leave with Jamie before we both died. But only a moment later another man shouted from the car behind me. "Fill your car with whatever kids you can and we'll get yours!"

A mother in front repeated the call, and soon we formed a bucket brigade, people tossing random children into cars and screeching off.

Homes were burning all around us. The main school building erupted into flames. Kids still wearing heavy backpacks began running down the street, no longer waiting for vehicles. The last school bus was near the end of the block. What looked like a young boy hanging onto the door fell into the street.

This couldn't be happening, I told myself for the thousandth time today, pushing a kid into the front seat of Nick's car. This couldn't be happening. How could this be happening? I just wanted to go back to my condo in Chelsea. Kick back with some weed and watch a fun movie. *The Hunger Games. The Day After Tomorrow.*

Jonathan had looked a bit like Jake Gyllenhaal.

Was he a witch? A demon? A devil? Who had put me in this nightmare of a life?

Maybe I was in a coma.

The heat was blistering. I could feel my eyes drying out. Tiny embers no larger than grains of sand pelted us like burning needles.

Jamie screamed.

I grabbed four more kids and crammed them in the back seat next to my daughter, slamming my door and pulling away. The smoke was now so dense I couldn't be sure I wasn't about to run over some other kid. I could see flames on both sides of the street, glowing through the thickening smoke.

"Don't let me die, Daddy!" Jamie shouted, her voice muffled as she shrunk onto the floor. I hoped her mother, whatever her name, was okay. The other kids breathed heavily but said nothing.

The car in front of me stopped, engulfed in flames. Two people staggered out, burning, and collapsed.

"Everyone down!" I shouted.

There were no atheists in foxholes, I remembered, but I still didn't believe in God. What kind of god would allow such a massacre?

And I was no savior, that was for sure.

In the rearview mirror, I saw the street behind me explode into flames. I steered to the side of the car blocking me, ran over a burning, writhing body, and gunned the engine, driving as fast as I could into more of the thick black smoke.

Section Two: The Man of Our Dreams

"Devo confessarti una cosa," the young woman gazing up at me said. She was short, little more than five feet tall, with mousy brown hair, thick glasses, and an endearing smile. She had a single dimple in her right cheek. "Ho baciato molti ragazzi."

I laughed. "Anch'io."

Patrizia frowned and stepped back. I closed my eyes and shook my head to clear it. I felt a dull headache behind my left eye.

What the hell was happening? A moment ago, I was in the midst of a blazing wildfire.

But that wasn't a moment ago. It felt like months had passed since then.

Had they?

Maybe I was still in the hospital in New York.

"Davvero?" Patrizia asked. "Sei…sei…?"

Aspetti. How was it that I understood Italian? That I even realized it *was* Italian? I also knew this woman was named Patrizia, that my name was David, though Patrizia liked to call me Davide.

Last time, I hadn't known anything.

Had that all been a dream? A TV show I'd watched?

One flew smack into the cuckoo's nest.

"Yes," I explained, still in Italian, "I'm…bisexual." I didn't want to ruin David's life, just as I hadn't wanted to ruin Nick's. Of course, I *had* ruined Nick's. I'd ruined my dad's. I'd ruined my own.

"But we're getting married in the temple tomorrow."

Where was the real David, I wondered? Maybe he'd return in time for the wedding. I needed not to fuck anything up before then.

I hoped he wasn't dead. I supposed. I mean, I didn't even know the guy. Except I did. I remembered the day he sprained his ankle learning to ride a bike. I remembered his high school graduation. I remembered his first day in the Missionary Training Center. Was he in Paradise now?

Perhaps he'd been zapped into the body of a stronzo being hit by a truck in lower Manhattan.

I took the young woman's hands and guided us both onto a bench. We were in a tiny park in Biella, the Alps spectacular before us. David had completed a two-year Mormon mission here several months back and returned to marry Patrizia, who'd also been a missionary in some of the same cities they worked. I had flashbacks of district meetings in Torino, church talks in Bergamo, working a streetboard in a public square in Milano.

Cioé, una piazza.

This jumping around into other lives could be a polyglot's dream, I realized, at least if I entered the mind of someone who spoke well. And assuming I remembered what I learned from one experience to the next. I remembered the name of Jamie's school, after all.

I closed my eyes again. Was that little girl and the other kids dead in the middle of that burned out neighborhood? What about Jamie's mother? All those other people whose names I didn't even know? I wasn't sure I wanted to look it up.

"I'm not bisexual," I clarified. "I'm gay."

Patrizia was silent a long moment.

"You must have suspected," I said. "You let me read your diary last night." Memories popped up as I needed them. That ability sure would have come in handy back in Superior.

Was this a practice-makes-perfect skill? Some kind of Hindu reincarnation thing?

Who in the world got reincarnated right into the middle of someone else's life?

"You wrote, and I quote, 'Non é l'uomo dei miei sogni.'" The real David might be gay, too, I realized, though you'd think I'd remember a thing like that. Only I had no sense at all of his orientation.

I'd heard of asexual people but frankly found the concept difficult to understand. But that would certainly make Patrizia's diary entry reasonable.

"Oh!" Patrizia's olive skin turned a shade pinker. I seemed to have a thing for olive-skinned women. Odd for a gay man, but then, what about all this wasn't odd?

"I—I just meant…"

"Yes?" That I wasn't the man of her dreams. There was little ambiguity in the statement.

"You aren't quite as handsome as I'd have liked."

I laughed again. I hadn't had a chance to look in the mirror yet, but there was no reason to doubt her.

"Non sei offeso?"

I shook my head. How could I be offended? Comments like that hurt only when you believed them. Inside, I was still the same person, that good-looking guy in Chelsea. Or that decent looking dad-bod guy from Colorado.

But I wasn't really either of them, was I? Or this guy, either.

I was what was inside. A bit of a prick.

More than a bit.

Which meant that as long as I was in this body, I had little going for me on any level.

"Sognerò di te stasera!" Patrizia promised.

I wondered how long I'd be here. Just a few hours, perhaps. Maybe a week? I looked over at the lightly snowcapped mountains, the sky above blue and beautiful. No imminent disasters looming. Might as well treat this as a vacation. The air felt warm, probably high 70s.

Or rather mid to upper 20s.

No one was about to freeze or suffer a heat stroke. Everything looked green, no dry underbrush on the slopes threatening our existence.

Were there earthquakes around here?

"Maybe we should sleep together," I suggested.

Patrizia stared.

"Just sleep. No sex."

Patrizia tilted her head slightly. "Are you teasing me?"

I remembered now that we'd watched *The Picture of Dorian Gray* a couple of evenings ago. I was staying in her parents' home along the Cervo, down the hall from her room. Patrizia's parents were still Catholic and none too happy that their two daughters had converted to a different faith. But their older daughter had married a local Mormon with a thriving wool business, and I'd agreed—David had agreed—to move to Biella so no one would be stealing her away. My brother-in-law Flavio had apparently given me a job.

"I will *not* miss out on a temple wedding," Patrizia insisted.

"You might want to try sleeping next to me *without* any expectation of sex," I explained. I didn't add, "even if the other David does come back."

She frowned. "Are you saying we'll never consummate our marriage?"

"Never is a long time." Temple marriages were for time and all eternity.

I seemed to know Mormon doctrine, too, more's the pity. Another flashback had me in Brescia to the east, working during a "zone bust" with Patrizia and another male missionary, Elder Taylor, assigned as my "companion." We'd approached a lovely young teenager and handed her a pamphlet. "La legge di castità."

How mortifying.

I wasn't sure why I felt mortified for something I hadn't done.

Religious conservatives always accused gays of recruiting. Even if the goal were biologically feasible, it would probably never be more effective than converting Italian Catholics to Mormonism. Still, it might be fun at some point to print a pamphlet of my own and proselytize the sexually devout across Salt Lake. "How to Break the Law of Chastity."

I hoped I didn't get zapped into some body in Utah.

"I want children, Davide. Lots of children."

"You can have as many as you like." I probably shouldn't even be giving this much of myself away but keeping everything secret hadn't worked particularly well last time. If Patrizia and I were getting married the next day, though, I'd have no trouble remaining celibate until then.

I wouldn't have had sex with the woman in Colorado, either, only she hadn't asked first. Of course, I could have said no, but I'd really had no idea what was happening at the time. I knew more now. At least a little. And I wouldn't take advantage of the situation.

Not that I cared about this stranger. There was no point caring about anyone. Never had been.

But I did *kind of* know her. I remembered two young women knocking Patrizia's scriptures out of her hands and walking away laughing. She hadn't even seemed fazed by the incident, just picked the books up, dusted them off, and smiled pleasantly at the next folks approaching along the sidewalk.

If I'd been zapped into David's body while he was still with Elder Taylor, though, the fact that I already kind of knew him might not have kept me from trying to get to know him more Biblically.

Or was that Book of Mormonically?

"The train doesn't leave until morning," I said. "I know your mom planned a nice meal tonight, but can we eat out instead?" We needed some unsupervised talk. Postponing the wedding would be humiliating for Patrizia, but I also didn't want to anchor her to a gay husband. No telling when the real David might come back. What if I was sucked away to someplace else and no one at all came back into his body?

Patrizia nodded. I could see in her eyes she thought I simply had cold feet. Lots of American missionaries promised to marry Italians but changed their minds once they returned to the U.S. I'd come back almost a month ago, though, to get started at the new job with Flavio. Mostly office work, keeping track of invoices. Surprisingly not as boring as it sounded.

Who knew that the wool market could be fascinating?

I'd thought "making it" in New York was the highest goal I could ever set, but just a few hours in these other lives had already shown me otherwise.

Though I did like Chelsea. And my office window did provide a great view of the Hudson. Those were great things, too.

The Lamborghini, though…

Mannaggia! They made those in Italy, didn't they?

"All right," Patrizia said. "I know a good restaurant." Her tone implied she expected me to break up in public where she wouldn't make a scene. But I knew Patrizia wouldn't have made a scene anywhere.

People often said things like, "I felt I'd known her for years the moment we met," but in my case, it was true.

Still felt odd.

"Patrizia," I said softly, "I want you to feel free to make a scene no matter where we are."

She tilted her head again.

"In a restaurant. At home. At work. At church." I paused. "In the temple…"

She gasped and covered her mouth with her hand.

During a slow, calm meal in the Rione Rossigliasco, I told Patrizia everything I knew about what was happening. After dessert, we headed down to the river for an evening stroll.

"It's beautiful, isn't it?" I said, gazing into the Cervo.

Patrizia reached up and touched the back of my head. And then the right side. And then the left.

No lumps transferred here from the fall in Colorado.

"You're not making all this up, are you?" she asked softly.

"I'm afraid not. But Davide might be back soon."

"I guess this is what it's like to meet one of the Three Nephites." Patrizia squeezed my hand. "We thought that only happened in America." We stood by the river in silence for several minutes. "I suppose it's no stranger than finding Lazarus come back to life," she said, "or listening to a donkey argue."

"We can still get married," I said. "The whole point of doing proxy work in the temple is that those who can't be there can accept the work done by people in other bodies. The marriage will still be valid after I leave and the real Davide gets back."

Patrizia sighed heavily, shaking her head. "Heavenly Father makes life so hard for members of the Church in Italy." She paused. "It's just that I really wanted…really wanted to…to finally…" She looked up at me and sighed again.

Oh my god.

"If it's okay for a soul in a body that isn't yours to make baptism and wedding vows in the temple for spirits who aren't present, surely it's okay if your real husband's body makes love to you, no matter who's inside him at the time."

Patrizia laughed, surprising me a bit. "You're just trying to give me a headache so I *won't* ask for sex tomorrow," she said.

"Is it working?" I asked.

She punched me in the shoulder.

I took her hand and we began walking again. Several other couples, even some entire families, strolled along nearby.

In Chelsea, people had places to be, places to hurry to.

In Colorado…who knew? I hadn't been there long enough. But it struck me as a place where you drove more than strolled.

I didn't want to marry a woman. I didn't want to marry at all.

I was living in a beautiful town, where people *strolled*, doing a job I should know nothing about but somehow did, and liked. All so different from last time.

I took in a sharp breath, and Patrizia turned to look at me. What if this happened ten more times? Thirty? I forced a smile back and we kept walking.

What if *this* was my final destination? I had better find a way to make this work if I didn't want to end up in an Italian mental institution.

Yikes. What if that was my next jump?

I started to say something but caught Patrizia looking at a cute guy walking alone. "Is he the man of your dreams?" I asked gently.

Patrizia blushed.

"To be honest," I said, "I wouldn't mind inviting him along on our walk."

The man was heading in our general direction, and as he drew closer, our eyes locked for that extra split second that could convey so much. Not gaydar really. More like a laser.

Gayser?

"Vorresti un po' di compagnia?" I asked.

The man's eyes darted quickly to Patrizia, and I saw a second look on his face that registered recognition. "Why not?" He stepped in between us and turned back so we were all facing the same direction, Patrizia on his right and me on his left.

I felt like Dorothy with the Scarecrow and Tin Man.

Only Dorothy was the main character.

So was I the Scarecrow?

The man's name was Stefano, and the only additional information he offered up front was his love of evening strolls. So Patrizia asked if he went to church regularly. He didn't. She asked if he'd read any good books lately. He'd read *Accabadora* and *XY*. She asked if he liked women. He liked everyone, he assured us. She asked what his biggest goal in life was. To die happy.

She'd have made a great bishop, I thought. Or job interviewer.

I wasn't sure who was guiding us, Stefano from the center or Patrizia from the side, but we ended up at the Giardino Shriver. Not much more than a field, really, but it overlooked the Cervo, and even at night, we could see the mountains not far away.

We chatted about inconsequential, forgettable things. I was concentrating mostly on Stefano's hand rubbing the small of my back. And the large of my ass. Patrizia gave nothing away, but it seemed likely she was experiencing the same attention.

"Do you prefer candied violets with or without chocolate?" she asked nonchalantly.

Stefano chuckled pleasantly. "Are you guys inviting me back to your place for a threeway?"

I appreciated that Stefano looked neither disgusted nor smug at the possibility.

"I live with my parents!" Patrizia said.

"So you guys want to come back to my place?"

"Dio mio!"

"Well, God doesn't belong *only* to you," he teased. "And if we can share gods, surely there are other things we can share, too."

I almost felt sorry for Patrizia. This had to be so out of her normal realm of interpersonal relationships.

But there was a glitter in her eye that wasn't fear.

"We'd love to," I answered him. "But we don't want to lead you on. There'll be no sex. Tonight. Patrizia and I are getting married tomorrow."

"A threeway tomorrow evening then?"

I motioned for Patrizia to close her mouth so as not to give Stefano any more ideas. She did so, lobbing a glare in my direction. "Let's just go back to your place for a bit and listen to some music," I suggested. "We're catching an early train in the morning."

Stefano considered a moment and then nodded. "I'm into Mahmood and Måneskin," he said. "But I expect you guys are more the Laura Pausini type?"

Several pleasant melodies flooded my brain in an instant. Laura Pausini was great.

"I like Francesco Gabbani," Patrizia said with a slightly defiant air.

Stefano smiled. "People say I could be his son."

"Are you?" I asked.

Stefano chuckled. "I *wish* he was my daddy."

***

Stefano's apartment was a couple's paradise, three love seats in a semi-circle like an amphitheater facing a stage consisting of a huge flat screen with impressive speakers set below, a stereo system to the right and a small fridge to the left. Just behind the abbreviated sofas was a large kitchen table.

He motioned for Patrizia and me to take the center love seat, while he plopped down in the one to our left, kicking off his shoes. I took mine off as well. Patrizia frowned but did the same.

Stefano grabbed the remote and a moment later, soft music filled the room. Someone began singing about "Musica leggerissima."

As missionaries, Elder Taylor and I hadn't been allowed to listen to worldly music, but we'd opened our balcony doors more than once to eavesdrop on the neighbor's radio. "Quando Fuori Piove" and "Come Nelle Canzoni" and many others.

We logged it as Companion Study.

The receptionist at Flavio's wool factory played Tommaso Paradiso and Lorenzo Fragola. And a surprising amount of Italian rap. I'd had no idea.

Neither Patrizia nor I said anything. Stefano fiddled with his remote again, and I seriously thought he might start showing us porn. Instead, we soon heard a lovely baritone voice singing "Eternamente Ora."

Patrizia smiled. "Thank you," she said.

"Prego."

Stefano lay down in his love seat, throwing his legs over the end in our direction. He waved one foot at Patrizia, who sat closest to him, the foot close enough to sniff if she'd chosen to. She shook her head, rolled her eyes at me, but then took Stefano's foot and began massaging it.

"You sure you didn't want the center love seat?" I asked over Patrizia's shoulder. "Then she could massage your right foot from the love seat you're on now and I could massage your left from the other."

Stefano's legs would have had to be a meter longer for such a thing to be even remotely possible. The image was so ridiculous we all broke into laughter.

"I knew it!" Stefano said. "You just want to spread my legs!"

Patrizia tensed but didn't stop rubbing his foot. I thought it best not to tempt fate any further.

The same baritone voice soon began singing "Spazio Tempo." Stefano sang along and only a moment later, Patrizia joined in. I almost felt like a fly on the wall but experienced no sense of jealousy. Why should I?

Patrizia continued massaging Stefano's foot, removing his sock. He motioned for me with his other foot, and I sat on the floor beside him and massaged the other. He told us about growing up an only child with a large extended family. Stefano enjoyed movies and television, falling in love with Mehmet Günsür, a Turkish actor who'd married an Italian woman. He would have been content with Michele Riondino, too, and invited us back to watch *The War Is Over* with him sometime.

"But you'd better tuck me in bed now," he said, "if you want to get any sleep before your train in the morning."

"I suppose you have a mirror on your bedroom ceiling?" Patrizia asked.

She *had* told me she'd kissed a lot of boys.

Stefano laughed and led us to his bedroom. He stood with his arms stretched out as if he were royalty waiting for his servants to undress him.

I realized I didn't know the word for "valet" in Italian. Must not have come up much in missionary work.

Patrizia unbuttoned Stefano's shirt and tugged it off while I unbuckled his belt and pulled down his zipper. In just a moment, Stefano stood before us completely naked. To his credit, he managed not to have an erection.

Given what Patrizia had said about my looks earlier, perhaps that wasn't the challenge I imagined.

Stefano sat on the bed and slid his legs under the sheet but then motioned for us to pull it up to his chin.

Gay or straight or bi, this all seemed unusually odd.

Since I was in a coma with severe brain damage anyway, who cared?

I looked over at Patrizia, shrugged, and leaned down to kiss Stefano on the forehead. She leaned over and kissed him on the mouth.

Then we headed back to her parents' place.

"Did you like your bachelorette party?" I asked.

Slowly, in English, she replied, "You are so flippin' annoying."

I squeezed her hand. "I love you, too."

***

Patrizia and I both wore green aprons at our wedding in Bern. I'd never been into cosplay before but supposed that was what my entire life consisted of these days.

Auntie Em must have stopped wondering what happened to me by now. But that was hardly something Patrizia needed to hear today.

We didn't have enough money for a honeymoon—just as well—though clearly there'd never be a Lamborghini in our future, either. So after the temple ceremony, a laborious two-hour ordeal that had nothing to do with either of us until the last few minutes, we headed right back to the train station.

Once we settled into our seats for the trip across the border, I pulled up a Francesco Gabbani video on my phone and tried to sing along. Davide had a decent enough voice. Though Patrizia didn't act enamored of it, she didn't appear pained, either.

"Devo confessarti una cosa," she said, turning to look out the window. I knew what she was about to say and waited without prodding her. I didn't have to wait long.

"I didn't dream of you last night." She turned back to me, not embarrassed or apologetic, not remorseful. No resignation.

"That's okay," I assured her. "I dreamed about you."

Now a mix of emotions rather than a lack of them registered on her face. "Davide," she said, "liars don't make it to the Celestial Kingdom." She squeezed my hand and then turned back toward the window.

"I don't need to be back at work until the day after tomorrow," I offered tentatively. "How about we give Stefano a call when we get back to town?"

"Oh, Davide," Patrizia said, resting her head on my shoulder, "do you think that's wise?"

"Sì, carina," I told her. "Penso proprio di sì."

***

Soon I was back working at the wool factory, which genuinely was fascinating, though Patrizia didn't care to hear any details. That was okay. I felt like someone learning to walk again after a serious car accident, learning to speak after a stroke. Everything was interesting, even Patrizia's discussion of the lessons she taught in Relief Society on Sunday, though she'd only reluctantly accepted the calling.

"Siamo amminstratori della terra, delle nostre comunità, delle nostre famiglie, e delle vite che ci sono state regalati."

It was delightful to listen to the words and realize I understood what she was saying. I sure wished I'd studied other languages more back in the day.

All this to say I didn't feel put out that Patrizia wasn't enamored of my day job. In the evenings, we listened to music in her room while we reviewed baby names and plotted ways to get the bishop of our tiny congregation to call Patrizia to work in the nursery. Or we chatted with her parents, which mostly involved me quizzing them about Patrizia's childhood.

When she was eight, she'd saved a friend who was drowning.

She'd read the entire *Decameron* at the age of twelve.

Thursday evenings Patrizia and I reserved for teaching immigrants Italian. I only knew as much as Davide did, which meant I still made mistakes all the time, but I could communicate, and that's what immigrants needed to do.

Monday nights were for Family Home Evening. And right from the start, we invited Stefano. Or, rather, we invited ourselves over to his place. We could hardly conduct the meeting to our satisfaction with Patrizia's parents hovering about. The first time, Patrizia asked me to present a short, spiritual message before we got to the fun stuff, but I did not want Stefano to feel we were proselytizing. There'd just been a devastating wildfire in China that had killed almost thirty firefighters in addition to an even larger number of local residents. I still hadn't been able to force myself to look up what had happened in Colorado, but I gave a brief talk about consequences.

"It's probability and outcome," I said, trying to remember a line I'd heard in an old Warren Beatty movie. "This isn't like drunk driving, though. You *could* get home safely even if you're drunk. But more of these fires are unavoidable if we don't stop burning so much oil." I cared and I didn't care. Like everyone else. I mean, everyone wanted to retire in comfort and luxury one day. And how could I not be sensitized to the subject after burning to death?

Dying caught a person's attention.

Patrizia frowned and Stefano looked a bit confused. "This is what Mormons do on Monday nights?" he asked.

"We do something to help the family feel like a unit," Patrizia said. "Work on an art project together, cook something for a sick neighbor and then deliver it together, whatever we feel is appropriate for that week."

"Am I the art project?" Stefano asked. "Or the sick neighbor?"

"We're going to play a game tonight," I said. "Something to help us get to know each other."

"You already know what my bare feet look like," Stefano said. "And my naked body. How much more intimately did you want to know me?" He raised an eyebrow and smiled.

"Ah," I said, "but you haven't seen *us* naked."

"Davide!" Patrizia drew her thumb across her throat.

"We're going to play Truth or Dare," I said. "Something I used to do in my Single Adults group back in the States." I remembered that Davide had always told the truth because he'd led such an innocent life and felt more embarrassed to accept a dare.

I asked Stefano to turn the radio on. While Irama sang "Ovunque Sarai," I handed out the first challenge. "Patrizia, Truth or Dare?"

"Truth!"

"Have we consummated our marriage yet?"

The gasp that ensued was so loud Stefano jumped up, thinking she'd choked on one of the hazelnut butter cookies we'd brought over.

"How—why—why—?" she spluttered.

"We can hardly expect Stefano to feel like part of the family if we keep secrets from him," I explained.

"There are secrets," Stefano interrupted, "and there is propriety."

"Oh, I don't think any of us believe much in propriety," I said. Stefano sat back down but looked at Patrizia with concern. "So, getting back to the game," I went on, "what was your answer, sweetheart?"

Patrizia gave me a glare but then turned to Stefano. "I'm saving myself for someone else."

Stefano leaned back into his loveseat, his eyes darting first toward the door and then to the balcony. Trapped in his own home by two crazy strangers.

"Since I answered the first challenge," Patrizia said, "now it's my turn." Her brows furrowed as she considered her options. "Stefano, Truth or Dare?"

"I don't think I want to do either," he said. "My hands are sweating."

"Truth or Dare," she repeated.

He sighed. "Okay. Dare."

Patrizia started to speak but then stopped herself as a new song began playing on the radio. "I want you to stand on your balcony and sing this Francesco Gabbani song as loud as you can."

While Stefano struck me as a man up for almost anything, he looked relieved at the rather tame demand. He opened the doors, faced the building across the street, and began belting out "Viceversa."

The rest of the evening went smoothly enough that Stefano accepted our self-invitation back to his place the following Monday evening.

Sometimes, Patrizia would begin with a five-minute "lesson," sometimes Stefano agreed to say something uplifting and, when pressed, Patrizia would agree to let me present a short homily. Remembering the structure of the tiny lessons Davide used to give at church growing up, I might say a few words about missed opportunities or about making choices we didn't regret or about making restitution when we did make bad decisions.

I cared and I still didn't care. So even with Davide's background to draw on, I couldn't speak for more than a few minutes.

Which was just as well because the main event of the evening was almost always Truth or Dare. Sometimes, we did cook for an ailing neighbor or congregant or coworker. Or we took long walks through the town. Or went to the cinema to see a movie. But mostly, we played.

I dared Patrizia to run up to Stefano on the street while others were nearby and beg for his autograph as if he were a star. Stefano dared me to kiss Patrizia's feet.

And Patrizia dared Stefano to take off his shirt and lie face down on his bed so she could massage his back.

Our bishop might not have agreed, but we managed to keep our friendship chaste. Everything was relative, of course. One evening, we played Spin the Bottle like teenagers. But we never went beyond deep kissing.

God only knew what Stefano was saying about us to his friends.

***

I was enjoying life, despite the celibacy. I knew I could justify fucking around if I'd wanted to. But knowing I *could* have sex helped dissipate some of the sexual tension. And it wasn't as if I didn't beat off most days.

Stefano had given *both* Patrizia and me photos of him standing shirtless beside his bed.

To be honest, I was more afraid of disrupting my surprisingly good life. The few times I dared watch the news, in addition to the normal political drama, there were reports of flooding in Florida and Scotland, wildfires in Australia and Argentina, category 4 hurricanes in Texas or category 5 typhoons in the Philippines, massive tornadoes in Mississippi and South Carolina. It was impossible not to feel I was being set up.

Maybe there was a god. And he/she/it was an ass. A talking donkey.

I'd burned to death twice, and I was determined not to let it happen again. I bought several fire extinguishers for Patrizia's parents and two for Stefano's apartment. I kept one beside my desk at work.

One Thursday evening after we came back from teaching, Patrizia sat silently on the edge of our bed in her temple underwear. "Do you think…?" she began.

"Yes?"

"Should we at least *try* to have a sexual relationship?"

I sat beside her. Perhaps our "garments" were the reason I'd managed to stay celibate. Difficult to see those when I unzipped and still feel attractive.

"I think you should ask Stefano out on a date," I said.

"Just the two of us?" Patrizia didn't sound alarmed at the idea.

***

Patrizia invited Stefano to see *Il Passeggero*, a period piccc based on a Jewish refugee's novel written just before the outbreak of World War II. They had a bite to eat afterward and took a long stroll near the river afterward.

A tiny part of me almost felt left out, but Stefano seemed to anticipate this and before he and Patrizia headed out sent me a video revealing him slowly removing his clothes and then pleasuring himself in multiple ways.

The three of us were still in this together.

Apart from the celibacy, I'd never had to worry about remaining faithful before. My relationships had rarely lasted long enough to progress toward commitment. Jonathan had had a casual self-confidence that made his average technique perfectly acceptable. The big dick hadn't hurt, of course. Stefano's was comparable but darker and uncut. Now that I'd seen it in action, I wasn't sure how much longer I could hold out for the real thing.

The past few months had been nice, just getting to know each other as people. But hormones were real, and something needed to give.

***

"Stefano," I whispered in the dark two weeks later, half an hour after we finished making love. Patrizia hadn't been thrilled about the fornication but reluctantly accepted it was necessary, perhaps more for Stefano's benefit than mine. She was at her parents' place tonight while I enjoyed my second sleepover in a week with Stefano.

We'd eventually have to incorporate Patrizia into the sexual aspect of the relationship, too, or it wouldn't be sustainable.

Stefano and I were still awake, his head resting on my chest. He liked listening to my heartbeat. Every couple of minutes, he gently squeezed my side to let me know we were still basking in an extended afterglow.

"Sì?"

"I can't believe how lucky we are to know you."

"I can't believe how lucky you are, either."

"Stefano." I caressed his thick hair. "Have I ever seemed…strange to you?"

He scooted up to rest his head on my shoulder and faced me, his warm breath massaging my chin. "Of *course*," he said. "You wouldn't be here otherwise."

I tried to chuckle but couldn't. I'd had no trouble when I'd first arrived telling Patrizia my secret because even though Davide had known her well, I really hadn't at the time.

"There's something you should know," I began. I was almost sure I could handle rejection but was afraid Stefano might break up with Patrizia, too. Yet the longer I delayed addressing the truth, the more likely the worst-case scenario would result.

"That your real name's Hunter?" he asked.

"What?"

"Patrizia told me weeks ago," he said. "She was afraid you'd dump me to avoid the discomfort of telling me."

"I see." Whatever feeling was coursing through me was unidentifiable.

"You're the Wandering Jew."

The term sounded vaguely familiar.

"Maybe the Wandering Mormon." He fingered my left nipple.

"I'm…I'm just a guy."

"I looked you up," Stefano went on. "You were killed in that car accident."

"Oh."

He took a deep breath, and I knew what was coming. "You died in Colorado, too."

I wasn't sure I could speak at all now. "I…ah…" I swallowed. "And Jamie?" Patrizia probably didn't even remember the other names I mentioned the day before our wedding.

"Davide." Stefano kissed my neck, and my chin, and my cheek. "You don't want to know any more than that. Let *me* keep some secrets."

I had to be dead, didn't I? No one like Stefano could be real. No one like Hunter/Nick/Davide, either.

Patrizia, though, she could be real.

I never thought I'd be able to love a woman.

Or anyone.

Stefano gently pushed me onto my side and then onto my stomach. He lay on top of me, his weight glorious. I thought he might penetrate me, but instead he adjusted the pillows and fell asleep lying on my back.

I stayed awake as long as I could to savor every last second of the luxury.

I didn't want to die.

And I didn't want people I cared about to die, either.

I hoped Jonathan had found a good man.

***

Patrizia sat on the center loveseat, Stefano's head in her lap, his legs hanging over the arm of the sofa. She rubbed his chest through his open shirt as they listened to music. "Occidentali's Karma" and "Volevamo Solo Essere Felici" weren't exactly slow songs, but the two of them looked so relaxed they might fall asleep.

I sat at Stefano's computer, emailing Davide's parents. His family weren't especially loving but were at least polite, and we emailed regularly the first Sunday of each month, though they didn't want to talk on the phone. Stefano's parents had moved to Venezia, so I had yet to meet them. Stefano, Patrizia, and I ate at her parents' house every Saturday, keeping Sunday dinner to ourselves. Whatever they thought about our friendship with Stefano, they never asked a single awkward question.

***

"You like Stefano, don't you?" I asked.

"That's not the point."

"He likes you."

"Davide, he's not even Mormon."

I shrugged. "Civil marriages aren't recognized in the temple, and temple marriages aren't recognized civilly in Italy."

Patrizia tilted her head slightly.

"You and I were married in the temple," I said, "and you and Stefano can get married civilly."

Patrizia put her hands on her hips. "How does that solve anything? I'll then be unfaithful twice over."

"No," I said. "You'll be completely monogamous with Stefano."

"But *he* won't be monogamous!"

"He doesn't need to be," I said. "He isn't making any temple vows."

"But you did!"

"Yes, and I'll remain monogamous."

"To him! The vow you made was with me!"

I shrugged. "You'll be monogamous. I'll be monogamous. The rest Heavenly Father will have to sort out in the Millennium."

Patrizia's head straightened, she closed her eyes, and she sighed heavily. Of course it didn't make any sense. Neither did much of the other theology that sprang into mind. But I knew we'd taught similar things as missionaries, telling mothers who'd had miscarriages that somehow "everything would be fixed" after the Second Coming and they would have the chance to raise their children then. Gays and lesbians would be restored to a "normal" sexual orientation. Unattractive people who couldn't find spouses would be made beautiful enough to have another chance.

I wasn't sure how anyone found such beliefs comforting.

I was no theologian—maybe next time?—dear Lord, I hoped there'd be no next time—but what little I had ever understood of any religion could only be pushed so far. At some point, the logic always broke down.

And yet people believed.

Patrizia nodded. "I can't help feeling you're leading me to hell. But I like you and I love him, so I guess I'm willing to be stupid."

"Love is always stupid," I said. "No one would get married otherwise." I remembered the look in Jonathan's eyes when I flipped him off at the dealership.

Patrizia frowned.

"What I meant was—"

"I know what you meant. And if I wasn't worried about keeping my temple vows, I'd ram my hand right up your ass."

I leaned down and kissed her forehead. "Oh, I think we should save that for our anniversary." She didn't smile.

Naturally, we didn't tell Patrizia's family about the second wedding, taking care of it in a city official's office with witnesses we recruited on site. But the three of us did live in the same apartment, a larger one in Stefano's building that at least made the move relatively easy. When Patrizia asked what she should tell folks at church who asked why, I said, "Tell them the truth. That it's none of their business."

"Any reason we make up," Stefano said, "will just lead to more questions. Best to shut it down right from the start."

"What if they think—?"

"They can think whatever they want." Stefano took her in his arms and kissed her.

"There are no church courts for what goes on in the minds of busybodies," I said.

Stefano alternated beds, spending one night with Patrizia, the next with me, the following night with Patrizia again, and so forth. He spent a fourth night with Patrizia every week.

My nights were Monday, Wednesday, and Friday.

I wish college courses had been as fun.

Not even someone as sexual as Stefano wanted sex every night, but the intimacy of sleeping next to someone I didn't worry was going to steal my debit card or hack into my computer was surprisingly nice. Not that I'd picked up hustlers often in New York, but even well-dressed guys in a professionals bar weren't always the most honest men around.

Geoff had pilfered my favorite Limoges pillbox, a red Maserati.

Patrizia cooked most evenings because she wanted to, so she also did much of the grocery shopping. Stefano and I divided up the remaining chores.

Patrizia liked puzzles, and we spent at least half an hour each evening at a card table, piecing together a castle in Germany, a hillside of homes in Cinque Terre, waterfront apartments in Amsterdam. We watched *Imma Tataranni*, *La Porta Rossa*, and *I Bastardi di Pizzofalcone*.

The first day I'd arrived in Biella, I'd worried the place was about to be struck by an asteroid or maybe a stray nuclear bomb meant for *FIAT*. Then I'd wondered if marrying a woman was the "disaster" I might face.

But the three of us never even argued.

All right. Once. I wanted a glass of wine and Patrizia vetoed it, saying Stefano could enjoy it for me by proxy. She'd resisted the daggers I glared her way with ease. I had to content myself later with asking Stefano to funnel a tiny amount of wine in through my back door. An activity that had held no interest for me in my Chelsea days.

But we adapted as we needed to. I paid my tithing to keep my wife happy. I sucked my husband's toes to keep him happy.

Patrizia had seen a terrifying documentary about global warming and insisted we only use candlelight at night. Of course, we still used the gas stove and still watched television, but we no longer used electric lights most of the evening.

If I lived long enough in this body or another, I'd probably be forced to make other adaptations.

But if I could adapt to carpools in Colorado and wool factories in Piedmont, I expected most of us could make whatever adaptations we needed in order to survive.

Like going to Biella's one karaoke bar with Patrizia and Stefano because they both liked singing solos and duets, and I loved to see them smile.

***

"Does my sperm taste different from other guys'?" Stefano slid his finger through the line of cum above his navel.

"Not sure what you mean," I said. "Every guy's cum tastes a little different. Even the same guy's cum tastes different from one day to the next. You know that."

Stefano nodded distractedly, still playing with the mixture of clear and white juices on his abdomen. "It doesn't taste…deficient?"

I leaned over and licked the still warm load off his stomach and then kissed him. After a few moments, I lay back down, resting my head on his shoulder. "What's this all about?" I asked. "Does Patrizia not like it?" It was often an acquired taste, after all.

Stefano didn't answer right away but finally managed to get something out. "I don't seem able to give her a baby." He breathed out heavily. "She really wants a baby."

"You only get pregnant the first time when you don't want to," I said. "It's a law of nature. Otherwise, it takes time. The right conditions."

Stefano reached over with his free hand and caressed my face. "The doctor says I have a low sperm count. I…might never be able to be a father."

He gave me a guarded look.

"Please don't say anything to upset her."

I nodded. "I understand the request, but it's probably not possible to talk about this even delicately without it being upsetting." I cupped his balls lightly. "Aren't *you* finding the discussion unpleasant?"

"Yes."

So I thought about it over the next few days, watched some videos, read a few articles.

I didn't pray about it.

I wanted to tell Patrizia she could have all the kids she wanted during the Millennium, but there was no point postponing happiness even if such things truly did come to pass. Whatever we were going to enjoy in life we had to make happen ourselves.

I knew she wouldn't consider sex with me, of course, apart from her lack of physical attraction. We'd made covenants, she believed in the Law of Chastity. Blah, blah. Blah, blah.

Since I cared for her, what was important to her had to be important to me, too, whatever I might normally have felt about it.

"We could get a sperm donor," I suggested one evening after dinner a couple of weeks later when I finally gathered enough courage to broach the subject. "The Church doesn't forbid it."

Patrizia twisted a strand of hair around her finger. "Yes," she said, "I did look into it. The procedure's supposed to be carefully regulated, but I couldn't be sure what I was getting."

"Does it matter?" Stefano asked. "Even if you had my baby, we might make a child with Down syndrome or autism or something else. We might have a child that got a mean gene. Neither of us has had our personal DNA mapped out. We don't know what we do or don't carry."

Patrizia nodded. "It would be embarrassing if my parents found out. Or people at church."

Stefano and I looked at each other.

"And you don't know how mortifying it is to get into those stirrups."

I thought it best not to mention slings or rimming or other socially inappropriate activities I'd participated in long ago, back when I was Hunter. Or even the cavity search I'd deliberately provoked once at a Chicago airport by joking about drugs, just so I'd have a suggestive story to tell at parties. We were talking about Patrizia's comfort level, not mine.

"What are your feelings about adoption?" Stefano asked. "There are lots of children already on the planet without families."

Patrizia nodded again. "It's hard to get infants, though, isn't it? And we'd wouldn't know if she spent nine months in the body of an addict or alcoholic."

"An older child?" I suggested. "Where we can already tell the general personality?"

Patrizia closed her eyes and put her hands on her head as if to keep it attached to her body. "I'm not shopping for a dog, am I?"

We let the conversation drift to other subjects then, but like so many things in life, when you tried to avoid a topic, it kept thrusting itself back into view constantly. There was a news report on Ethiopian orphans. A report on child trafficking out of Brazil. The image of dead men, women, and children floating face down after an immigrant boat sank off the coast of Malta. A report on in utero gene editing

But we still avoided resuming the conversation.

***

Since our second marriage, every evening had pretty much become Family Home Evening, but we still tried to make Monday nights just an extra bit special. Truth or Dare could only be sustained by folks who didn't know each other well, so we adapted it to a "You can ask me *one* question about anything you want" at the end of the activity. That allowed us to feel vulnerable, a necessity, I'd realized, and helped us understand the annoying idiosyncrasies each of us naturally possessed.

But during the bulk of each Monday evening, we read to one another. Family time wasn't unlike hosting a book club. We each presented a book we were interested in, voted for a selection, and took turns reading chapters and then discussing them. When that book was finished, the other two whose book hadn't been chosen on the previous round got to make another proposal, the same book we'd wanted before or a different one if our mood had changed over the past several weeks.

Sharing a book that only we and perhaps no one else in our circle had read created a lovely intimacy, made the three of us part of the in-crowd. Since we could discuss the latest chapters at any point during the week, at home or not, making allusions and references gave us a secret language only we understood.

***

"Davide's been to the doctor," Stefano announced one evening over dinner.

Patrizia stopped moving with a forkful of pappardelle halfway to her lips, alfredo sauce dripping onto her plate.

"His sperm count is normal," Stefano added. He'd told me he wasn't going to bring it up yet.

Patrizia put her fork down.

"You can use some of Davide's sperm while still obeying the Law of Chastity—"

"How?"

I pretended I wasn't part of the conversation and shoved some pasta into my own mouth. But it must have still seemed staged when Stefano leaned toward me and licked a drop of sauce from my chin.

"I'll give him a blow job in the other room so you don't have to be part of that sexual encounter."

"Yes?"

"Then I'll come to our bedroom and go down on you."

I swallowed before I finished chewing. And sat like I was watching television.

"Mannaggia la miseria," Patrizia muttered.

"Then I'll push it in a little deeper with my fingers."

She fixed her eyes on his hands, resting next to his dinner plate. They looked larger than I remembered.

"And then we'll make love and see what happens."

***

It was early April, almost a year since I'd arrived in Davide. Patrizia was two months pregnant, mildly grumpy only when nauseated. She, Stefano, and I went for an early Sunday morning stroll along the river, high at this time of year with the snow melt, the air brisk but not cold.

"Want to go swimming?" Stefano asked. "Maybe get a massage?"

"I want a warm bath," Patrizia informed him.

He looked up toward the mountains. "I bet we could get a room cheap up in Oropa," he said, "now that the ski season is winding down." He looked at us both hopefully. "At least if we go on a Monday evening."

"Still sounds more expensive than a bath at our place," Patrizia said.

"But we don't have a heated swimming pool," Stefano pointed out. "Or a hot tub."

Patrizia stopped walking and looked at him. Stefano then threw one arm over her shoulders and another over mine. "You guys go on to church and I'll get online and set things up."

"That's very generous of you," I said. We had three separate checking accounts, one joint checking account, and a joint savings. Treats always came out of our personal accounts. "Sounds wonderful."

"Shouldn't we be saving for a rainy day?" Patrizia pulled Stefano's hand from her shoulder and kissed it. "Maybe we could—"

"We're having Family Home Evening tomorrow night in Oropa," I said.

Stefano kissed me on the cheek and then kissed Patrizia on the lips. Biella wasn't a big town, but while we tried to be reasonably discreet, we weren't going to make ourselves miserable.

That was also our policy at the hotel the following evening. Stefano and I both left our workplaces early, and the light rail to Oropa took barely twenty minutes. The three of us enjoyed an early dinner, took a long, slow stroll afterward, and sat on a stone wall overlooking the valley while we read a single chapter of our current book club selection.

We ended up back at the hotel just after 10:00. Patrizia gazed up the hill toward the sanctuary and murmured softly. "Too bad you both have to be back at work in the morning."

"Doesn't mean the night's over," Stefano said. "I still want to go swimming."

"I'm not sure I can fit into my swimsuit."

"You haven't gained even a single etto yet, Patrizia."

I pointed out the back window of the lobby. "No one's in the pool right now."

We changed quickly and headed back down with our towels. The air was decidedly chilly, so we climbed into the pool as soon as we set our things on some chairs. Stefano ducked under the surface, popping up almost a minute later with his trunks in one hand.

"You're going to get arrested," Patrizia warned.

"Want to share a cell with me?" He playfully tugged at the edge of her swimsuit and she stuck out her tongue. He rushed over and sucked it into his mouth. While she held onto the side of the pool with one hand, her other reached deep below the surface.

Stefano broke away, grinning, and swam from one end of the pool to the other while Patrizia and I glided a few feet from the deck, treading water in the deep end. When Stefano returned, he brushed his feet against my legs and kissed me full on the mouth.

After a few minutes, Patrizia tapped Stefano on the shoulder, and he swung in her direction to make out with her for a while. She then reached out for me, and the three of us treaded water for the next twenty minutes, taking turns kissing.

I'd read somewhere that there were scientists who believed the universe was a hologram, that none of us were "real." I suddenly wondered if I was a glitch in some incomprehensible being's video game.

Maybe my character had gone up to the next level.

It was certainly better than the level I remembered as my first.

My dad—Hunter's dad—had brought me to the YMCA once to teach me to swim. The lesson consisted of him throwing me into the deep end and watching me splash about in terror until a lifeguard jumped in.

Back in the locker room, he mocked my scrawny body—I was eight—in front of several other men.

When I complained to my mom later, she'd simply said, "If you don't want to drown, then learn how to swim."

Even as a child, I'd found it odd she thought the possibility of drowning had been the most distressing part of the incident.

I never let them know when I finally did learn.

Stefano had the biggest, widest, longest tongue. It felt like heaven in my mouth.

I heard footsteps and turned to see a couple in their fifties walking out onto the deck. I swam noisily a few feet from Patrizia and Stefano to give him a chance to grab his trunks without their eyes on him.

We headed back to our room, rinsed off the chlorine, and climbed into bed. Stefano had chosen a room with only one. He slept in the middle, and the three of us spooned and cuddled through the night.

Nookie was off limits, but it was still the most satisfying sleep of my life.

***

Neither Patrizia nor Stefano asked much about my previous lives. I wasn't sure either of them ever truly believed me, but then, what sane person would? They tolerated what they probably saw as either a delusion or fabrication, and while that might have come across as patronizing (or matronizing), I only ever felt good will from both of them.

All right. Perhaps Patrizia had a few sharp words for me now and again as her pregnancy developed. Nothing I didn't warrant.

I wasn't sure what I had done to deserve such good fortune. I felt a bit like a woolly mammoth brought back from extinction with frozen DNA, a leukemia patient restored to health with stem cells.

I'd had a shitty life in New York regardless of my upbringing because I'd been a rather shitty person. I'd never paid much attention in school to the Nature versus Nurture debate, and I had no idea how that played out when I had both a different body and different circumstances in these additional lives.

It still felt weird to say "lives." I caught myself once in a while staring at others in town, or at work or at church, wondering if any of them might be in similar "switch" situations. I watched people on the news. But if someone ever seemed off, there was no way to pin down why. Had their spouse said something mean to them? Had their boss? Did they have a toothache? Had they skipped their meds?

It seemed unlikely that whatever phenomenon was overpowering my life would only affect one or two people on the entire planet, but if this was happening to anyone around me, they weren't stupid enough to let on.

Early October brought dark clouds and rain but no snow. Patrizia was due in two weeks, and all three of us grew more excited by the day.

"Are you sure?" Stefano asked for the umpteenth time. "You're okay with my name as father on the birth certificate?"

"We don't know whose sperm made it to the finish line," I replied, also for the umpteenth time. "If the genes are yours, you *should* be listed as the father. And if they're mine, that will still give me whatever 'claim' I need. We both have marriage certificates, after all."

Patrizia had already made it clear that she wanted Stefano's name on the document. He just wanted to be absolutely, doubly, triply, umpteenthly sure we were all still equal partners in the relationship.

For Family Home Evening the following Monday, I handed Patrizia and Stefano a greeting card. On the front was a photo of an ancient olive tree. On the inside, I'd written, "To the best two out of three parents a kid could ever have."

Patrizia smiled but Stefano looked at me intently. "The third wheel on a three-wheeler isn't superfluous," he said, reaching for my hand.

Only nine more days until the official due date, though we were all nervously aware contractions could begin any minute. We had our emergency bag by the front door. The "lesson" tonight was going to be another drill on delivering a baby ourselves if necessary en route to the hospital.

The day had been dark with thick clouds, and now that the rain had begun in earnest, it felt even darker inside. We hoped to get through two chapters of our current book tonight. With twenty candles set up throughout the living room, with what it took to make and store and ship them, I wasn't sure we were decreasing our carbon footprint even a toe's worth.

It felt good to try, but when I saw heavy rain like this, or last night's news report of a late season hurricane striking Boston, and new wildfires in Argentina, I wasn't sure feeling good was very useful.

Patrizia sat on the center love seat, with Stefano on the one to her right and me on the other. The arrangement had worked in Stefano's former apartment, so we'd kept the set up the same when we moved in together all those months ago.

We had history.

Patrizia quizzed us what to do during a breached birth. Stefano asked her to clarify the procedure if the baby had aspirated meconium. I encouraged Stefano to practice breathing with me.

Rain thundered against the windows. It almost sounded like hail.

"Let's stop," Stefano said before Patrizia asked her next question. He moved over and sat beside her. I sat on the floor at their feet.

"What about—?"

I held up a hand and she stopped.

That rain was *loud*.

It was impossible after what happened in Colorado not to worry. So much time had passed since then, but in the back of my mind, I was always aware I might have been doomed from the start. At best, I might wake up from my coma. At worst, Patrizia might choose only Stefano and divorce me.

"I can't see what's happening," I said. The rain flowed down the glass in such thick sheets we couldn't even see the balcony.

Stefano took the remote and tried to turn on the television, but there was no power. It might have gone out two hours ago for all we knew. Patrizia picked up her cell phone and then shook her head.

"Do you think everything's all right out there?" she asked. One hand instinctively rubbed her protruding belly.

"The riverbed's wide," I said. The Cervo was officially called a torrent because it raged both spring and fall, dwindling down to barely more than a trickle sometimes in the summer. But because of that wide variation in level, no one built right next to the embankments. The Corso Lago Maggiore passed high over an empty chasm half the year.

I stared at the windows, wondering how I'd know if we were in danger. I remembered years ago reading a Titanic survivor's account. She'd felt a vibration in the middle of the night and knew immediately something was wrong, gathering her children and hurrying to the lifeboats before any emergency had been declared. She was one of the first people to deboard the ship.

"How about some karaoke?" Stefano suggested.

The karaoke machine had been my gift for his and Patrizia's first anniversary.

"No electricity," Patrizia reminded him.

"A cappella karaoke?" He grinned.

Patrizia began with a sweet version of "La vita davanti a sé." Laura Pausini at her finest.

Stefano followed with "Puntino Intergallatico." I hoped we'd all get to a Francesco Gabbani concert one day.

Or at the very least, they would.

Then I sang "Adon Olam." In Hebrew. Realizing for the first time I must have been Jewish at some point. Too bad that hadn't happened before I met Jonathan.

When *had* that happened? And why was I only starting to remember it now?

The rain thundered outside.

Was that a secondary roar beyond it? The river? There'd been mudslides near Zumaglia last week.

Patrizia sang again. I'd never heard her without accompaniment. She wasn't bad.

Stefano followed with yet another song, dancing along with the lyrics. He was rather good, too.

Maybe I just liked listening to them.

I passed on my next chance to sing. The only lyrics that came to mind were from "Les feuilles mortes," and I didn't want to sing that.

Damn. When had I been French?

"Why don't you guys sing a duet?" I suggested.

Stefano had barely crooned three words when we felt the building shudder. He stopped and put a hand on Patrizia's stomach. She put her hands on his.

"You guys stay there," I said. "I'm going out to the balcony."

I squeezed through the doors as quickly as I could to keep the downpour from drenching the candles. The rain was so heavy I felt I was looking through fog, though perhaps the problem was more the lack of streetlights and illuminated apartment windows. Still, I could make out the river.

My mouth fell open again.

I closed it quickly. The rain tasted funny.

Trees flowed downstream, random boards and chairs. A Vespa.

A car.

I couldn't be sure in the gloom and from this distance, but what looked like a body face down rushed past. Probably just a log, I decided. Or maybe a piece of furniture.

Yes. That next lump was almost certainly a mattress.

Distant parts of town still had light, but it couldn't penetrate far in the deluge. It gave me hope, though, that our power could be restored once the rain let up in the morning.

Lightning flashed, and I saw for a brief instant the face of a woman clinging to something in the water.

The cold rain soaked into my chest.

I watched as the ground nearest the river collapsed into the raging water. Further upstream, I could barely, barely detect the outline of an apartment building a couple of blocks away.

Then I didn't see it anymore. But I felt another tremendous vibration. The roar was already so loud, though, it could hardly be amplified any further.

I squeezed my way back into the apartment. "We need to leave," I said. "Now."

Patrizia and Stefano didn't even ask why. We quickly walked four floors down to ground level. The lobby was covered in twenty centimeters of dirty water.

Stefano and Patrizia exchanged glances. I motioned for them to wait by the stairs while I made my way to the building entrance. Peering outside, I saw that the street itself had already become a river. Only a few feet deep, but the water carried a van, miscellaneous pieces of splintered wood, bottles, chairs, trash bags, a dog. And people.

Their shouts were muffled by the roar of the rain and water.

I remembered video I'd seen once of the Indian Ocean tsunami. Only the folks here were almost invisible in the dark.

Ghost casualties.

We weren't walking out.

I waded back to the stairwell, shook my head, and we started back up the stairs. A couple of neighbors peeked cautiously onto the landings as we passed, but no one said a word.

"We…we should pray," Patrizia said once we were back home. Then she sniffled and wiped her eyes. "We haven't been sinning," she said. "We haven't." Stefano nuzzled her neck while caressing her stomach.

"Maybe we should go to the roof," I said. "Hang onto something lightweight. Maybe some cushions." Neither of them heard me over the thundering patter against the glass.

The building shook again.

"Hunter." Patrizia's voice pierced the roar. She hadn't called me that in almost a year and a half. "Hunter, take us with you."

She was crying openly now, hugging her belly. We'd asked the doctor not to tell us the sex of the baby, looking forward to the surprise. Our son would be named Gabriele or our daughter Chiara. Patrizia had even agreed that my room would be reserved for the baby, and I'd moved into the main bedroom two months ago.

People adapted as they had to.

"Hunter," Patrizia begged, "please."

Stefano's dry eyes told me he understood fully what was about to happen. If either of them had ever believed my story at all, they had to have known all along the danger of being involved with me. Yet they'd willingly accepted me into their lives, anyway.

"I love you both," Stefano said. He kissed Patrizia's stomach. "I love all three of you."

Patrizia shook her head. "No, no, no, no, no."

A roar louder than anything I'd ever heard descended down the valley.

The building shook once more. And started to tilt. Several of the candles still lit fell to the floor and went out.

I couldn't hear Patrizia over the deafening rumble, but I could read her lips, the words the same in English and Italian.

I looked into their eyes for an eternity of seconds before the last of the tiny flames were extinguished and I was blinded by falling, soul-crushing debris.

Section Three: Tomorrow Is Another Today

A bare-chested young man in white pants was dancing on a rock jetty while another young man filmed him with a camera attached to his chest like a newborn baby.

"Please get back on the path," Manuel told them.

Wait, did *I* just say that?

The young man in the white pants continued dancing.

"You need to get back on the path," I said.

But I wasn't the one saying any of this. I was…I was Dennis Quaid inside Martin Short, Raquel Welch inside Jean Del Val. I was an evil spirit possessing a herd of swine.

Or at least taking over the body of some *tonto lamentable* working in a public garden.

"Oh, no problem," the young man with the camera attached to his chest said. "We didn't know."

Was "herd" even the right collective noun for pigs?

I could feel irritation rising inside me, Christopher Walken after donning a headset handed to him by an annoyed Natalie Wood.

"That information is posted on our website," Manuel said in a surprisingly calm tone. "It's also on the sign at our ticket window. And you had to step past the sign telling you to 'Keep on the path' and then step over the rope fence to walk out onto the jetty."

I could feel his inner struggle to remain "professional" and wondered if he could sense a hundred other thoughts flying through our mind at the same time—"We didn't know it was cheaper to make public transportation free than make it impossible for those on assistance to find jobs." "We didn't realize old growth forests were being shredded for toilet paper." "We didn't understand the postal service was being sabotaged by politicians who wanted to privatize it."

I was almost sure I'd been a scientist at some point. Or at least a teacher.

Maybe a journalist?

An inmate spending as much time in the prison library as possible.

Oh my God. I suddenly remembered inmates screaming, corrections officers, everyone crowding into the showers as flames tore through our building.

"We hear you, we hear you," the dancer assured me. "You don't have to bitch anymore."

And Manuel didn't, but I could hear his thoughts, could feel his weariness, could sense he was still unaware of me. If the young men were telling the truth, it only meant they were so unconcerned with others they couldn't conceive that a notice announcing guidelines to protect the commons might exist in the first place.

Even Sybil's multiple personalities had been separate. Mine seemed all jumbled together.

Sybil's case had been manufactured to create a bestseller.

But at least it had given Sally Field her first real chance to shine as an actress.

Manuel held back an urge to grab one of the young men by the ear. I could see my fingers twitching in anticipation. Had he done that before? Had I?

I was Arnold Schwarzenegger in *Total Recall*, trying to figure out which memories were real.

I didn't know who this Manuel guy was, but he sure spent a lot of time watching movies. People used to make references to Greek mythology. Now our allegories came from studios.

Several more scenes flashed through my mind, thirty thousand people buried by mudslides in Venezuela, fifty thousand suffocated by the heat in Russia, five million killed by a pandemic after an ancient pathogen was released from thawing permafrost.

Who in hell *was* I?

Two of the three deaths I remembered most clearly had been caused by weather disasters, but I wasn't sure whoever or whatever was putting me through all this was trying to teach me "a lesson." It seemed more likely that given the severity of the climate catastrophe, whichever life I ended up in would be affected by it to one degree or another.

I followed along as Manuel headed back to his ticket booth. What other choice did I have? But as we sat ringing up the next customer, a thick fog entered our head. I vaguely noticed that the skin on our hands was wrinkled, the hairs on our arms gray.

He was an old man.

Maybe I was senile.

Were we having a stroke?

All I could see before me now were white mists drifting past white clouds.

Was I dead?

I heard tapping. Then more tapping. The noise continued, and I was finally able to make out some words. "You okay?"

Two elderly women peered into the ticket booth through a window at the counter.

"I'm sorry," I said. "Was that two senior tickets?"

"You're not going to ask for our ID?" One of the women laughed. The other still looked worried.

I managed a smile and finished the transaction as quickly as I could.

Manuel was gone. I was alone in here, though I still wasn't sure where "here" was. A tiny, cramped ticket booth, sure, but where? Why?

And what had become of my predecessor?

I could still remember admission prices for this private garden, the prices for our T-shirts and postcards and magnets. I remembered I had an old Ford Escort out in the parking lot. I remembered I could speak Spanish, but not very well.

My family had been in Texas for two hundred years.

A middle-aged white woman in a wrinkled sun dress, with bleached blonde hair under a wide-brimmed hat, strolled up to the window sucking on a purple ice pop.

Not allowed in the garden.

"What a cute dog," I said, smiling at the woman's black toy poodle. "Is that a pet?"

"His name's Teddy."

"I'm afraid we can't have pets in here, but I can recommend several good areas nearby where pets are welcome."

Instantly, the woman's face grew a shade darker. "I just saw a dog come out!" she said loudly.

Manuel might be gone, but I still had access to some of his memories, like journals or emails I could flip through at will. Like Marilu Henner remembering every day of her life as if it were last Friday.

I certainly seemed able to retrieve Manuel's TV and film trivia. I could even remember—

Dio mio! Cos'é successo a Patrizia e Stefano?

Why was I wasting my time worrying about admission guidelines?

"What you saw was me turning away someone trying to come in with a dog." It was Manuel's standard answer in these situations, and I said it as casually as he did.

In time, I might end up liking Manuel and his life, but nothing could ever replace the loves of my own. While the woman continued ranting, my eyes locked on a pair of scissors in a mesh pencil box on the counter, and I knew that if killing myself would reunite me with my family in Italy, I'd stab myself in an instant.

I watched my fingers twitching and resisted the urge to walk out. I had work to do. I couldn't let Manuel get fired.

A young couple exited the garden, with a tiny terrier sporting a huge pink bow on its head and straining at its leash. Not the behavior of a service animal. They'd probably slipped through while I was addressing the jetty dancers.

"Well, *they* brought a dog in!" the woman exclaimed victoriously. "If *they* can do it, why can't I?"

Where was a raging wildfire when you needed one?

Even a stray bolt of lightning would do. A bit of turbulence.

I remembered my plane going down somewhere over the Pacific in unexpectedly severe weather.

Dozens of Manuel's memories suddenly surged through my mind like floodwaters, taking precedence over the others, the way vivid dreams faded so quickly after waking we couldn't even recount them five minutes later. I saw visitors to the garden smuggling tiny dogs inside their purses. Hiding a reflecting screen or other photoshoot equipment in a shopping bag. Stuffing food under their jackets after reading the "No Food or Drink" sign.

People got in with coffee sometimes, too, and other items that could stain the paths or cause damage or disruption to the carefully manicured park.

"Last week," I said to the woman clutching her toy poodle as if I'd threatened to rip it out of her arms and eat it, "a man threw a rock at a dinosaur skull in the Witte Museum."

"My dog is well trained!"

"Do you feel like running up to the ticket counter at the Witte and yelling, 'I want to damage a fossil, too! It's not fair that *he* gets to damage fossils and I don't! You're discriminating! *I* want to damage exhibits just like everybody else!'"

The woman stared at me in horror, as if I were unhinged.

The woman clutched her dog even more tightly, making it whimper. As they backed away, they were replaced by the next group in line, a weary grandmother with three young kids, all likely to inflict more damage than the dog ever would.

I looked at my watch. I wanted to go home.

To Sofía?

What I wanted more than anything was to drive straight to the airport and buy a one-way ticket to Italy.

Some memories never died.

I hoped.

***

"Honey," Sofía cooed, "you're drenched."

I pecked her on the lips. Manuel's car didn't have AC. In San Antonio. In the summer.

My wife was in her early sixties, with enough salt in her salt and pepper hair to cause hypertension. Which she probably did have. She couldn't have been five foot five yet almost certainly weighed over two hundred pounds.

I'd finally looked at myself in the employee bathroom mirror before leaving that first day, two weeks ago now. I might be a few inches taller than Sofía but easily weighed forty pounds more.

"Electricity went out at work."

"Why didn't you come home early?"

"They wouldn't let us leave." The ticket booth wasn't even shaded by trees.

"You don't think we'll lose *our* power?" Sofía looked up at the ceiling as if the answer were hidden behind the popcorn coating.

My wife had COPD but wasn't on oxygen yet. Our neighbor Thuc, however, was. His wife had died a year before of a heart attack, their kids and grandkids far off in Houston and Dallas and Chicago. Sofía checked on him once a day.

Our only child, Carlos, had been killed in a school shooting, a month before graduation, two decades ago. Manuel hadn't said his name in years.

"Well, come in, come in," Sofía urged. "I've got the fan set up, too. Cool off before you have a heat stroke."

News reports the previous evening claimed that more than three hundred people had died of the heat in Texas over the last few days. Mostly old, fat people. Several pets locked in cars. And a few children.

I'd looked up Italy my first day in Manuel's body. Even before leaving work that day, I could see from the date on my computer that the flood and mudslide hadn't happened yet, and I was too confused to know if any of my life in Biella had been real. If it was, Davide was with Patrizia and Stefano at this very moment.

How could it be possible? Should I look them up and warn them?

Warn *me*?

How, really, could I tell anyone at all?

And what if I tried contacting them and discovered my family *wasn't* real? That would even be more traumatizing than dying had been.

I wanted to see Patrizia's baby when it was born. Hold the infant in my arms.

Somewhere along the way, in one life or another, I'd learned about Occam's Razor. The most likely explanation for the impossible memories in my head was the simplest— I was certifiable.

But if Patrizia, Stefano, and Davide *were* listed…

Sofía took a flexible blue gel pack from the freezer and placed it on my forehead as I sat in front of the fan. "Ahhh," I moaned. "Better than an orgasm."

"What?"

Oops. It turned out that Sofía wasn't much of a talker. She listened every evening to an account of my workday over dinner, and then we settled in front of the television. She liked reruns of *The Good Place*, but the show only had two good seasons. The third season was so-so, and that last season, in the real heaven, was hell to watch. An eternity of everything going your way, with no obstacles, forever and ever and ever.

Of course, even the Medium Place had only offered an eternity of mediocrity.

Watching four, or five, or six episodes of the show every evening with Sofía was painful, but I refused to sequester myself in the spare bedroom—Carlos's room—to watch movies without her as Manuel had done.

He'd lost his factory job trying to deal with his grief over the shooting all those years ago, had drifted from mediocre job to mediocre job ever since.

"Sit here on the sofa and I'll set dinner on the coffee table," she said.

Sofía first set out some iced tea, black with peach and ginger, and another iced gel pack which she slipped into a large bib with a pocket. We often wore them on hot days to cool down our chests.

The old Hunter in me wanted to make a snide remark about Double D iced gel packs getting a woman's nipples perky. But someone else inside me countered with the observation that men's iced gel pack underwear might be worth considering as part of company uniforms to cut down on sexual harassment at work.

Chilled lettuce, tomato, and cucumber salad, with croutons and feta, was almost as comforting as the fan.

"Did…did you want to have sex again?" Sofía stared at her tea before picking up her glass and taking a sip.

We hadn't had sex once since I'd arrived. I was still as gay as ever, and I wasn't sure an elderly woman would have done it for me even if I weren't. At least if I still felt as young as I believed myself to be.

Only I didn't feel particularly young anymore. And I didn't sense much sex drive of any kind. Heat, humidity, and low testosterone were not remotely curative for grief.

Though the fatigue of constantly walking on dangerous ground couldn't be ignored, either. "Um, how long has it been?"

"Three years?" Sofía whispered. "Four?"

"Oh my god." No wonder we watched reruns of *Reba* and *The Nanny*, too.

Though neither of us laughed much at the jokes.

"I'm sorry I'm fat," Sofía mumbled.

I hissed in frustration and she flinched. "Don't say that!"

Not only because Manuel was no Greek god, either. I could see a pity fuck looming in my immediate future, but I wasn't sure what I felt was truly pity. This woman filled up the oatmeal container every day while I was at work, so it was full when I opened it the following morning for breakfast. She filled up the plastic cereal container, too, so there were always oat rings ready for a late-night snack before bed.

With the lactose-free milk she made sure was chilled a half hour in the freezer first.

All I ever did was get the coffee ready before bed so I could turn the pot on just before waking her in the morning with a kiss as I was heading out the door. Pretty much my only contribution to the relationship.

And still more than I'd contributed in most of my relationships back when I was Hunter.

I set my salad bowl down, stood, and pulled the coffee table aside. I turned the fan up a notch and knelt in front of Manuel's wife.

We both still wore our blue gel pack bibs.

I lifted her skirt.

"You should have warned me," she said, distressed. "I'd have taken another shower."

"Close your eyes, honey, and feel the breeze of the fan on your face."

I carefully worked Sofía's underwear down and buried my face and tongue in her for the next fifteen minutes. It wasn't even maintenance sex. More like maintenance appreciation. It mattered. I'd have a stern talk with Manuel one of these days…only I expected never to meet him again. When Sofía finally made the sound Manuel's neurons dimly remembered as a signal of success, I stood back up and pulled the coffee table over again.

"There's no reason we can't do that a little more often, is there?" I asked.

"It's so hot, Manuel."

I knew she was referring to the temperature inside the house, unable to counter the scorching heat outside, even with electricity.

"I think you're hot, too," I said.

She shook her head, embarrassed. But smiling.

***

The following day at work, I cranked the AC up as high as it would go, which only exacerbated the collective drain on the power grid. Our electricity went out just after noon.

The phone still worked, though.

"Can I rent the garden for my dog's first birthday party?"

"Can I be lowered into the garden by helicopter and propose to my girlfriend?"

"Can I donate my cat's poop for you to use as fertilizer? You'd have to come pick it up."

I turned away a group of teens in swimsuits who wanted to splash around our koi pond. And some college students with a beer cooler.

Lauren, the weekend cashier, found a homeless man sleeping in the public restroom when she opened up last Saturday morning. I'd been too lax checking the stalls at the end of my shift the previous day to catch that he'd chosen to be locked in for the night. Two days ago, Koyuki, the head gardener, chased a man from the gardeners' shed who had sneaked in to take a shower.

So many unhoused people, in tents and cars and even just sleeping bags. Who could blame them for trying to cool off? Or stay clean?

"We're losing a lot of our plants," Koyuki said this afternoon, hanging around the ticket window a few extra minutes, though the cool air that sometimes seeped out through the cash crack was long gone. "Even with the sprinklers."

"Do the timers work when we lose power?"

She shook her head. "It's all manual. But it's not like there's much other work we can do. It's too hot to move out there. Dan and I are here at 6:00 in the morning to beat the heat, but we can't get here at 4:00, can we?"

"You think we'll close?" I asked. I needed my paycheck. Sofía had given up her part-time job at Catholic Charities when it became too difficult to walk.

Neuropathy from the diabetes.

"That won't stop the heat."

The morning news reported that three thousand people had died in France from the heat over the past few weeks, another two thousand in Germany. Temperatures across much of India were 50 degrees Celsius.

I didn't need to look up the conversion anymore.

"Sofía told me the price of chicken is going up. Too many chickens dying."

"Farmers are losing cattle, too."

And a huge swath of corn country in Iowa had been devastated the other day by a derecho. Orange trees in Florida were being crippled by a new fungus.

I wiped my brow. "I don't think I can take this heat another five hours before close." Our boss didn't provide us with water bottles, though I brought a reusable bottle from home every day. He even turned off the water fountain near the public restroom, afraid it would attract too many "undesirables."

Koyuki looked toward the parking lot. No one was heading our way. "Why don't you put a Closed sign up, pull the gate half shut so the folks already here can get out, and take a cold shower in our shed?"

"Oh."

"If two or three people sneak in without paying, it's not the end of the world."

I wasn't sure our boss would agree, and I hardly wanted to be caught with my pants off if he made one of his rare surprise visits.

Maybe I should take a cold shower with Sofía this evening. We didn't need to have sex each time we wanted some intimacy. It was too hot to hug.

I nodded and found a laminated sign in one of our cabinets. Koyuki walked into the garden to check on the sprinklers or pull a few weeds in the shade or whatever else she could do. The gardeners' shed was dim, in the shade and with only a single light bulb in the tiny shower area. I stripped, stepped under the nozzle, and turned on the cold water.

I steeled myself not to shout, not one of those fools who jumped into freezing lakes to prove my manhood. A hot tub at the bathhouse was more my thing. I'd proven my manhood there many a time. But the water today wasn't truly cold. Perhaps a few degrees cooler then lukewarm. Yet still soothing.

I didn't hear Dan come in. He must have been standing there while I let cool water run down my ass crack, my fingers spreading my cheeks wide as I sought some comfort.

Assholes could be really hot.

"You look so relaxed," he said, making me jump. "I hate to intrude, but I'm filthy and feeling a bit faint. You okay if I come in for a minute?"

Only after I nodded my permission did he remove his soiled clothing and step under the showerhead with me. A couple of inches taller than I was, he had sandy hair and a tattoo of a rake on his right shoulder blade. He put his face up into the stream for a long moment, then dipped his head down to let the water beat the back of his head.

"Ahhhh."

I fumbled for a shriveled bar of soap on a caddy and ran it over his back and arms.

Was this normal? I'd never done anything similar even in a bathhouse. Manuel didn't seem to have memories of intimate interactions, platonic or otherwise, with Dan or other men. In another life, I might have found the situation odd, but I had learned to go with the flow. If that flow was soapy water sliding down the gardener's back, so be it.

Dan lifted first one leg and then the other for me to wipe down as well. But he gently took the soap from me to lather up his pubic hair. Then he handed it back before leaning against the wall so I could lather up his ass.

We didn't speak. Dan simply turned and adjusted as necessary so I could finish cleaning him. Then I turned off the water and we let the last drops slowly slide off our bodies.

He was fit and I was fat.

I didn't even know if he was gay. Or simply didn't want to wait for me to get out of the shower.

I lifted one of his arms and sniffed his pit. "All good," I said.

Maybe I could generate some cash for Manuel and Sofía by actually patenting that gel pack underwear idea.

Dan chuckled and reached somewhere into the darkness before handing me a towel and grabbing another for himself.

"Maybe now we'll get through the rest of the day," he said.

"I hope so."

"I heard the city may start rationing water."

"Not a drop of rain in the seven-day forecast."

"The white oak in the northeast corner is already starting to die. I've been working hard to save it, but…"

Now I felt guilty for wasting so much water in the shower, and for hoping Dan and I might spend even more time in there.

Maybe I'd buy some wet wipes on the way home to reduce bathing time over the coming days.

But the Escort was so hot, and when the stoplights went out just a block away from the grocery and I saw two cars miss each other by inches, I continued on home without shopping.

***

While Dan and I didn't shower together again, the smile he gave me every morning suggested we'd bonded in a way we hadn't before. I was no longer just the old man sitting at a cash register all day while he did the real work of maintaining the garden. He joined me on the wooden bridge one afternoon while I fished a visitor's phone out of the pond and playfully lifted his arm for me to smell his armpit.

"Yikes!" I said, making him laugh. But damn if that didn't get me hard.

Still, no communal shower.

"What was that all about?" Koyuki asked as I passed her on my way back to the ticket booth.

"He thinks he's funny," I said.

"Is he?"

I smiled. "Sometimes."

Koyuki raised an eyebrow, but that seemed to be the end of the discussion. We all had more pressing concerns.

Last week, a county order had been issued forbidding folks from washing their cars or watering their lawns. So far, that didn't affect the garden since we were a business, but we needed rain *now*.

It was no easier taking care of my own lawn with almost everything dead.

The power company had instituted rolling blackouts across the entire region a few days later, and the garden began closing two hours earlier to avoid the late afternoon roasting.

I bought extra gel packs for the fridge and freezer to help keep our food safe when we lost power. We also switched from buying frozen food to canned goods.

But we still wanted to keep our milk and cheese and eggs cool.

And no one wanted spoiled potato salad.

Sofía made sure Thuc had all the backup batteries he needed to keep his generator running during the blackouts. Water pressure was low because kids with no other way to stay cool opened hydrants to play. The city began turning the water off in different parts of town, these areas on odd-numbered days and those on even-numbered ones. Four hours at a stretch.

Not surprisingly, something about Manuel's life felt empty and pointless. I still hadn't figured out why I was here.

Probably because there wasn't a reason.

After dinner, I handed Sofía a bowl of frozen grapes as we sat down to watch another episode of the *Selena* mini-series. Getting her to try a new show had required some coaxing, but she'd consented after I agreed to a "real" kiss every morning before I left the house and another before we retired for the night.

Sofía and I were halfway through the second season. I hadn't realized Spanish was Selena's second language. The most shocking part of her story wasn't the murder but realizing how much effort and sacrifice had been required on the part of so many others to give the young woman even a fighting chance at success.

It made the battle over gun regulations seem almost insurmountable, the odds of implementing universal healthcare astronomical.

Understanding my presence inside Manuel downright impossible.

"More things in heaven and earth, Horatio…"

As Hunter, I'd never read Shakespeare, and I was sure David hadn't either, that Manuel hadn't. Nick, maybe, but would he have been able to quote the guy?

If I was going to be bombarded with stray memories from the minds of others, why couldn't they include the President's social media passwords or the combination to the safe at the Swiss National Bank?

I choked on a frozen grape and Sofía casually slapped my back. When it didn't help, I felt my face grow hot and saw terror in her eyes. She grabbed a photo album from an end table and smacked me on the back again, as hard as she could.

We didn't have many friends and rarely went on vacation. Most of the photos were of Sofía puttering about the house or me struggling with yardwork.

A lone grape shot out across the coffee table.

"You okay?"

I rubbed my throat and nodded. "Thank you," I whispered. Though choking to death didn't seem much worse than my other deaths. It would just mean starting over again from scratch. And, sedate and timid as Sofía could be, I liked her and wanted to stick around a bit longer.

"What happened?"

I could hardly tell her that if "the universe" had any specific plan by putting me into her husband's body or any of the previous ones, it was fatally flawed. Because unless I ended up in the body of a prime minister or CEO of a news network or scientist trying to splice the empathy gene into sociopaths, there was little I'd ever be able to do about anything that mattered.

The realization had caused me to gasp at just the wrong moment.

"We can watch the rest of this later," Sofía said. "It's too intense anyway. Let's watch something light. *The Woman in the House Across the Street from the Girl in the Window*?"

"Why don't I give you a massage?" I countered. "Rub your back. Your feet."

Sofía frowned.

I stood and held out my hand, trying to ignore my enormous stomach and the dribble of grape juice on my shirt. "It's too hot for clothes, anyway."

Sofía looked about as if worried someone was secretly filming a reality series. "I—I've got some baby oil in the bedstand."

***

An algal bloom in the koi pond killed half the fish before the gardeners could get it under control. Another oak tree died. A brush fire on the edge of town destroyed six homes and proved that PTSD endured through multiple lifetimes.

Several grocery stores in the city consolidated locations because they didn't have enough generators to sustain refrigeration at multiple sites. Texas was notorious for the deep freeze disaster a few years earlier when huge parts of the grid collapsed during a freak winter storm. The same infrastructure was no match for the heatwave, either.

And Texas was used to heat.

But it had been over a hundred degrees almost everywhere in the state for four weeks straight, absolutely unheard of, and even before that, much of the state had been in the upper nineties. Dallas had hit 113 yesterday and Austin 110.

It was 107 today in San Antonio.

Unbearable without air conditioning. Even poor folks who did have electricity could only afford fans and were suffering heat strokes.

In the last month, over seven thousand Texans had died of the heat, a thousand people in Oklahoma and a few hundred more in other states. The only thing all this searing heat was good for was solving decades-old mysteries—cars with the skeletons of missing teens found in evaporating rivers, long-suspected murder victims found in lakes and reservoirs across the western U.S., stuffed in barrels or chained to weights.

The discoveries hardly felt victorious.

Driving to and from work without AC was indescribable. I wore gloves so I could touch the steering wheel. I carried towels to place on the seat.

I also brought a change of clothing because my shirt and underwear were soaked by the time I arrived at the garden. Wearing damp underwear in this heat was not advisable.

Koyuki decided to use all her saved vacation to get through the month but would need to return next week, still mid-August. Dan started arriving at 5:30 every morning to do what little he could. The temperatures were unsafe by 10:00. If the garden's owner ever stopped by to check on things, it was only for a few minutes twice a week when he came to pick up the deposit. No more surprise visits in this heat. Almost all communication was via email or phone, with an occasional virtual meeting. If the computer was up.

"The only good part of the power going out every day," Dan said, stopping by the ticket booth just after 1:00, "is that you can only accept cash. That means fewer visitors. Which means less damage to the garden."

"It also means less income for the place," I pointed out. "Which makes our jobs less secure." We were closing at 3:00 every day now, four full hours before we usually did in the summer. The first half hour of each morning, if we had any electricity at the start of the day, I pulled cash out of the safe and officially entered it into our Point of Sale before sealing it in a deposit bag.

Lauren, the weekend cashier, had quit two weeks earlier. That meant I had to come in every day now, but since it was the only way to make up for the shorter shifts, I had little choice.

"Dios mío," I said. "Look."

Dan turned to see what I saw—a man around forty leading two elderly, painfully white people in walkers toward the entrance. Hatless in the blazing sun.

"Someone's hoping to get their inheritance early," Dan muttered.

I shook my head. "Two more hours before we can close."

Dan walked back for the gardeners' shed, which was only minimally cooler but at least out of the direct light. 3:00 eventually arrived with no 9-1-1 calls, and I locked the front gate. Checking the public restrooms, I caught a glimpse of myself in the mirror. Manuel's image always came as a shock. Even when I looked deep into my own eyes, I couldn't see *me*.

But I could sure see Manuel's excess weight. When I'd gone home my first day as the cashier, I discovered that Sofía had covered all the mirrors in the house with cloth, apparently months or even years earlier. Not out of mourning for our son but to avoid being forced to see what had become of her body over the years.

I suppose that was mourning, too.

While it was one thing to pretend I was sitting shiva, there were still plate glass windows in the world. And mirrors in public restrooms. It wasn't that Sofía refused to leave the house. She went shopping, we went to movies now and then, she went to church on occasion.

But the rare times she mentioned her excursions into the world, she would pick absentmindedly at the waist of her skirt or pants as she talked. She ran her fingers through her hair as if trying to fix a recalcitrant lock.

Since Manuel's excess weight wasn't really my fault, there was no reason to take the disgusted looks I encountered personally. Of course, the weight might not have been entirely his fault, either. Or Sofía's hers. It was like assigning blame for a skier's broken leg on the skier. Yes, if they'd chosen a different lifestyle, they might not have broken their leg, but no one gloried self-righteously in their pain. "You brought that multiple fracture on yourself. If you were a good person, you'd never have slipped on the snow." I'd seen that look of disdain on my father's face often enough to feel angry on Manuel's behalf.

Almost murderous on Sofía's.

The massages were helping but could never make up for years of emotional damage. At least she'd finally removed the cloth from every mirror last week.

I headed to the gardeners' shed hoping for a coolish shower before facing the blistering, miserable drive home.

"Oh, hey, Dan," I said. "Thought you'd already left for the day."

"My place gets too much late afternoon sun," he said. "I decided to bring a book." He shrugged. "Not like I can watch TV at my place or get on my computer."

The power outages were causing havoc with gas stations, too. People forgot that you needed electricity to pump. I'd considered staying overnight at the garden once or twice a week to save on fuel, but there was no sofa, no place to get comfortable.

I wasn't quite up to sleeping on the bathroom floor just yet.

"Mind if I take a shower?" I asked.

He motioned generously toward the stall.

I tried to be quick about it, both to conserve water and to avoid further coworker awkwardness. I'd need another rinse when I got home, anyway.

People forgot, too, that you could only do laundry if you could turn on your washing machine. And if the water wasn't shut off. And that in this heat, one needed to do a full load almost every day.

I turned away from Dan to wash my dick. Sofía was happy enough with the solo attention, but the last few days, she'd begun insisting on some reciprocity, surprised, I think, to discover she could still find Manuel's heavy body attractive, too.

When I turned around to do a final rinse, Dan stepped into the shower. "It's okay?" he asked.

After I nodded, he reached for the soap I'd just put back in the caddy and handed it to me. He turned around and waited for me to lather his back. Then he reached behind to guide my hand to his ass. After I pulled the slender white bar over his cheeks, he reached back once more and pulled them apart to offer me direct access to his crack and hole.

Whatever had happened before *might* have been "normal," if we were plotting on a bell curve and that experience was marked on the lower part of one of the slopes. *This*, however, could only be plotted somewhere far along the flat line at the bottom of the graph.

As much as I cared for Sofía, thirty seconds in the shower with Dan was doing more for me than anything at home the past few months.

Dan turned around and lifted his arms. It was difficult to get close enough to soap up his pits, what with my protruding stomach and his protruding dick, but I managed. I washed his arms and chest and abdomen. Then Dan guided me to his pubic hair before resting both hands on my shoulders.

I sudsed him up, but when I pulled away, he took my hand and placed it back on his cock.

"Bees are dying," I said. "Butterflies, too."

"What?"

"Pesticides. And antibiotics for livestock are killing good bacteria in the soil. Vegetables need those bacteria to provide nutrients. And to protect them against disease."

Dan pulled back and started laughing.

"'No' works, too," he said.

I'd also read that additional carbon in the air meant vegetables created a higher sugar content. Even healthy foods were less healthy as the climate warmed. The jury was out on the resulting effect extra carbs and loss of good bacteria in our gut had on the obesity epidemic. That might still be influenced by some as yet unknown virus.

Perhaps something else released by the thawing permafrost?

Why was I in San Antonio, I asked myself for the hundredth time. I felt like the grandfather in *Moonstruck,* crying because he was so confused.

Sofía had agreed to watch the old movie with me last night instead of another sit-com.

"I'll tell my wife everything I remember about your body," I said, "while I'm massaging her with baby oil."

Dan had never seemed interested in a relationship. I wasn't sure even now if he was gay or simply horny. And I was not at all certain I was up for finding a third partner again. But I felt almost refreshed thinking it might at least be possible.

Dan grinned and handed me a towel as I turned off the shower.

I was covered in sweat when I pulled up to the house. The waiting list for freon was months long, even if I could afford car repairs, and the house was so stuffy the AC had clearly been off for hours. The coffee table was set with a banana, a nectarine, and a Bosc pear on each plate.

Lots of carbs. But some fiber, too. And "trying" mattered, regardless of the outcome.

Two tiny, barely there ice cubes floated timidly in a pitcher of water. I shouldn't have stopped to buy that bottle of hand lotion on my way home. I just thought it might keep less heat trapped on Sofía's skin after a rub down than the oil.

"Sofía?"

I'd broached the subject of pegging last night, and she'd agreed, surprisingly quickly, to try her fingers first, eager to examine several equipment options online as well. Not even all gay men like penetrating other guys.

"Sofía?"

I'd sexted her before leaving work and hoped I hadn't scared her into running off to a friend's house. She'd told me weeks ago that she always headed to the confessional after I went down on her. The priest had assured her she wasn't sinning, but she could never be sure.

So I'd give her another chance to examine her conscience. Sometimes, she could examine it twice in a row.

Sofía wasn't in the bathroom or bedroom, not sitting on the back patio, which suffered direct sun at this time of day. Miserable even to pull the curtain aside to peek. Her car was in the driveway, though, so she may have popped in next door to check on Thuc. I filled my glass from the pitcher and guzzled the whole thing down before heading back out the door.

I tried ringing the bell before remembering the electricity was out. Then I knocked. When Sofía didn't answer, I knew there was serious trouble inside. Thuc was probably dead. More bodies were being found throughout the city every day. If he'd only been in a bad way, she'd have called an ambulance.

I turned the knob. The fact that the door was unlocked confirmed my suspicions while offering me some relief. Better than thinking she'd become confused in the unrelenting heat and was wandering about the neighborhood. The living room was stifling, dark with all the curtains drawn shut.

There was a faint smell of ammonia in the air.

"Sofía?" I called out.

I peered into the bedroom and saw them.

Thuc was in bed, the backup battery still powering his now useless oxygen. Sofía lay on the floor, lifeless as well.

Carlos had drowned in his own blood.

I shouted.

The air was so terribly thick, like breathing a steaming, wet blanket. I ran to open the window, trying to get some ventilation. But it was stuck, probably not opened in years.

"Sofía!" I called again. Maybe she'd just passed out. It wouldn't take much. We were all on the verge every day.

I tugged and pushed and tugged, finally getting the window up a few inches but really hurting my shoulder in the process. Mannaggia! I rubbed my left arm and rushed over to my wife.

"Please, please, please, please, please."

I knelt beside Sofía but didn't have the strength to turn her onto her back. I must've pulled a damn muscle.

It was so hot in the room. And my goddamn arm. That must be the flippin' rotator cuff.

"Sofía!" I called once more, my thoughts suffocating, as if the heat had wrapped its hands around my throat, my brain, my very essence. The mudslide in Biella was still months away. Perhaps I'd be back in time for it.

I hoped Jamie had survived the fire, even if I didn't.

I really wanted Warren to be okay. And Pavel. And Burak and Soren and Nzinga. And Brindabella, who'd drowned trying to save our mother.

I fell across Sofía's feet just as the world turned black.

Section Four: Keep Your Chin Up

I was holding a tiny paper cup full of meds. My first sensation was one of relief. I wasn't dying. Not right now, not this very minute. Looking up, I saw what appeared to be a nursing station. A long hallway with an empty wheelchair parked along one side ran off to my right, another to my left. The smell of antiseptic filled the air.

I had survived the heart attack.

I was genuinely surprised. Sofía and Thuc obviously weren't doing well. We weren't *all* being zapped from life to life.

If even I was. It was still possible I was in a coma somewhere in Chelsea.

I gasped, without choking on a frozen grape. *Maybe I was awake in a hospital in Manhattan right now!* I might be me again!

I set the cup of meds down on a tray and felt my face, my stomach. My breasts.

Uh-oh.

I vaguely remembered having been a woman before but the realization that I wasn't Manuel any longer was still disconcerting. I'd just been thrust into yet another life where I'd be dying again all too soon.

Who on God's green earth was in charge of this rebirthing program? I wanted to file a complaint!

Call the Midwife!

Still assessing my body, I discovered a nametag on my shirt. On my blue scrubs, that is. I tilted the nametag and read it upside down. Adeline.

Was the universe trying to teach me that life was futile? That it was pointless to try? To care? Why even bother teaching such a lesson, I thought, when that attitude came so naturally anyway? Everyone was bitter and cynical and resigned by the age of thirty these days.

Extra opportunities to fail weren't going to teach me anything I didn't already know.

Other than a dozen languages, livestock auction protocols, the most efficient way to harvest apples, nautical rules, garbage picker do's and don'ts, and other tidbits I'd incorporated, none of which would probably be useful where I was now. A sign on a door read "Restroom" and showed figures of a man, a woman, and someone in a wheelchair. I was in an English-speaking country again.

Or at least an English-speaking building. I supposed this might be a military medical center overseas. I seemed to remember an Air Force base in Greenland.

An olive-skinned woman in scrubs walked by. I'd never noticed how many olive-skinned people there were. She paused at what appeared to be a patient's door, knocked lightly, and went inside. The atmosphere in the hallway felt somber. Perhaps this was a cancer ward.

In most of my lives, I didn't see much possibility for "making a difference." Was the lesson simply to enjoy life while I could?

I thought I'd been doing that even back in Chelsea, though admittedly what I considered enjoyable had changed a good bit since then.

Was I being primed to recognize a chance when I saw it?

I remembered Jake Gyllenhaal in *Source Code*.

I was Franka Potente in *Run, Lola, Run*.

The bigger question remained—even if I could recognize a chance, what was I supposed to do with it?

"Better get a move on with those meds, hon," a black woman said, sidling up next to me.

"Oh, uh, yes. You're right."

This wasn't just a medical facility, I started remembering. It was a nursing home with lots of very old, sick residents. And I was…Adeline Daigle, an LPN. Forty-six years old. Sober for the last nine of those.

Without a mirror, I couldn't be sure who I was when I first arrived in these bodies. I often needed a drivers' license, a TV or computer or newspaper, to tell me where I was, what language I spoke. I'd been a young girl watching my family drown during a cyclone in Bangladesh, a truck driver in the Democratic Republic of Congo whose fuel tanker exploded. I'd been cleaning oil-covered seals in Alaska when the coastline burst into flames, led koalas to safety during a wildfire in Australia.

I'd watched my daughter drown in a flash flood in Germany, been celebrating my quinceañera when a mudslide wiped out my village in Bolivia, been held hostage by terrorists while working at a nuclear power plant in France.

I'd died of starvation during a famine in Sudan, and I'd watched my husband burn to death in our driveway while he waited for me to run out of the house so we could flee before the flames arrived.

That time, I think I'd been in Canada. BC, maybe?

And I'd lived brief, horrible lives in the Solomon Islands, in India, Saudi Arabia, Brazil, Kentucky, Indonesia, Japan, the Philippines, Nepal, Arkansas, Iran…

I looked down the nursing home hallway, remembering my assigned patients here, my nursing duties and skills. Each time I resurfaced in another body, the world felt like a box of puzzle pieces dumped on a table, but slowly, over the next several minutes, the pieces starting snapping into place, faster and faster the closer the puzzle grew to completion.

After making my rounds, I approached the nurses' station. Rosa and Shalandra were speaking in low voices, their heads close, looking worried. "What's up?" I asked. I was remembering now that Shalandra had been assigned a heavy patient not lucid enough to follow instructions.

"Azriel's a Category 4," Shalandra said. "It was barely a Category 1 this morning."

We'd just finished distributing the 10:00 p.m. meds.

"It's too close for us to get out," Rosa whispered.

And there'd be no shift change until daylight.

"Azriel," I said, thinking hard. We could already hear the rustle of leaves in the branches overhanging the nursing home. "I remember that one. It's…it's early June, right?"

Rosa and Shalandra stared at me. Shalandra was an RN and Rosa a CNA. Twenty-two residents lived here. Another had died last week. We were expecting a replacement any day.

"What I mean is, I remember the list of names for this year. And hurricane season has just started."

That wasn't what I'd meant at all.

"What do we do?" Shalandra asked. "We're so close to the water."

I remembered we were in Morgan City. "This is going to end poorly." Yikes. Had I said that out loud?

"What?" Rosa's head swiveled back and forth as if watching a pickleball match. "My kids…"

"I wouldn't be here if this was going to end well," I said.

Rosa and Shalandra stared at me again. Then Shalandra seemed to make up her mind. "Let's start moving the residents out."

"We'll get fired!" Rosa squealed, so loudly that even Ms. Peniston without her hearing aid must have heard. "There's the oxygen, the meds. We might give patients heart attacks!"

The sound of rustling leaves was suddenly drowned out by the pounding of a heavy downpour. The lights flickered briefly but remained on.

Rosa put her hand on her chest.

In one of my previous lives in another part of the country, Hurricane Azriel had hit at a time when I was overwhelmed, so I couldn't remember the specifics. Only that the storm surge had been far higher than expected and almost eighteen hundred people had drowned.

Nothing like what happened when I lived in Fiji. These were numbers that might have seemed fabricated only a few years earlier but which now felt almost unnoteworthy.

Death tolls didn't tell the whole story in any event. Even if a particular disaster "only" killed thirty-five people, another two or three million might be deeply impacted, dealing with washed out roads and bridges, with ravaged homes and schools and businesses. They might be without food or water or electricity for weeks.

Carlos's school shooting had faded from the news within days.

The storm in Fiji, at least, wouldn't happen until sometime next year. Those folks were still living their *Bridge of San Luis Rey* lives. I seemed to be fluctuating back and forth within a two- or three-year time span. Unfortunately, knowing the future never seemed to help. At some point, surely, it had to. Knowledge was power.

Wasn't it?

"Shalandra's right," I said. "We can't very well move people upstairs." Our facility was all on the ground floor. And we weren't getting anyone up on the roof.

Rosa rubbed her hands nervously as if disinfecting them.

"Call your husband," Shalandra ordered her. "Tell him to get your kids to safety."

While Rosa grabbed her cell phone, Shalandra and I locked eyes. I knew her oldest son had been killed during a routine traffic stop a couple of years back. Her daughter had moved to Atlanta to attend Spelman.

I was lesbian this go-around. But my wife had died of ovarian cancer a year ago.

I only worked thirty hours a week, so my job didn't provide health insurance. Melanie had worked full-time at the supermarket—one of those frontline heroes during both pandemics—but her insurance didn't cover early screening. Or two of the treatment options that might have saved her.

Shalandra was usually scheduled to work fewer than thirty-six hours a week to make sure she didn't qualify for benefits, either, and had been written up once when she worked an additional four to cover a nurse who hadn't shown up for the morning shift.

"Emile didn't even bother coming in tonight," Shalandra said. "Always a supervisor with our best interests at heart."

"He's got kids at home, though," Rosa pointed out.

"So he's a walking 'Baby on Board' and we get fucked?"

Rosa flinched.

"Let's get some calls out for ambulances," I said. "See if we can transport everyone to a hospital that's got a few extra floors."

Shalandra nodded and picked up the phone. She waited, said a few words, was put on hold and waited some more. Rosa and I stood silently beside her, listening to small branches slapping against the side of the building. I saw the Call light go on for Mrs. Guidry's room and groaned. She had an "emergency" at least twice each shift, even in the middle of the night. I was just about to head down the hall when Shalandra began speaking again.

"I don't care," she said. "You need to get over here. I—"

The lights flickered once more.

"Listen," Shalandra said, "we're not just anybody. We—"

The building began vibrating. A far-off rumble grew to a tremendous roar over the next fifteen to twenty seconds, fast, I supposed, yet it still seemed to take forever. It was that moment after you trip when you understand you're not going to be able to regain your balance, those terrible seconds between realizing you're going to hit the ground unprepared and the moment you finally make contact with the sidewalk.

We could hear limbs cracking outside, debris hitting the side of the building, glass breaking. The vibration grew so strong I wondered if it was an earthquake. It felt and sounded like we were in a rocket about to lift off a launch pad. Then the lights went out altogether.

"Get down!" I shouted.

We took cover as best we could, hearing thumps and bangs all around us but unable to dodge what we couldn't see.

Within seconds, the tornado had passed. I didn't feel any rain. The roof was intact.

"You okay?" Shalandra asked.

"Yes."

Rosa sobbed her response. The three of us helped one another up. The building was completely dark, not a stray beam of light anywhere.

"No emergency power?" I asked. Not even the Exit signs were lit.

I remembered we were two months late changing the batteries in the smoke alarms.

"I'll send a stern email," Shalandra said.

I could hear an old woman shouting somewhere down the hallway, an old man, too. Confused voices, not injured. Though still difficult to hear over the roar of the rain. It was coming down hard. The roads would be flooded soon, with or without a storm surge.

The last birthday gift Melanie had given me was a set of oil change ramps to lift the front of my car eight inches when heavy rain was forecast. I'd used them twice already since she passed.

They were at home in my garage.

I hoped my gray tabby would be okay. Never a cuddler, Gina had stayed beside Melanie every day those last few weeks.

"Should we try to get all the patients together?" Rosa asked.

"Why?" Shalandra fumbled for something and a moment later shone her cell phone in our direction. A quick assessment showed little damage indoors. Most of the sounds we'd heard had been on the roof, though I could see a dark void at the end of the hallway where a window had broken.

"So they're all ready when the ambulances come."

There was a moment of silence. Except for the roar of the wind and rain.

"No one's coming for us," Shalandra said.

"But…but…we need *help*!"

I reached out for both of them. Rosa instinctively pulled away from my touch. "Listen," I said, "we're okay for now, but this place will be underwater before morning."

Rosa whimpered.

"We've got three cars," I continued. "We can't get everyone out, but we can get a few. The ones with the greatest chance of surviving a rough night."

"What if there's a tree across the road five blocks away?" Shalandra asked. "I don't want to be stuck in a car when that storm gets here."

"It's not like we're in the middle of a marsh," I said. "We're in city limits. We just need to reach a multi-story building."

"If we leave people to die," Rosa sobbed, "we'll be arrested! I don't want to go to jail!"

"We're not the goddamn captains of a ship," Shalandra spit out. "There's nothing in our job description demanding we're the last to die." She hmphed loudly. "Or the first."

So many details of my previous lives were fuzzy, the deaths often the fuzziest memories of all. There were times I'd been alone, times I'd been left behind, times I'd died alongside friends and family and strangers, but never times when I left others behind.

"These are old, sick people," Shalandra said. "What good will it do them or anyone else to die with them? I want to see my daughter get married next month."

I'd been sixty years old in previous lives. Seventy. Even eighty. And my death had *always* felt premature.

Of course, I'd never had a stroke or needed my feet amputated. Or had Alzheimer's.

Not that I could remember.

But I'd always been attracted to men, no matter who I was.

Shalandra set her phone down and clicked away at the computer. "Internet's out," she said. "No cell phone signal, but at least the phones'll give us light."

"Mrs. Guidry's ambulatory," I said. "And Mr. Gonzalez is in pretty good shape. We can get them out."

"Ms. Boudreaux, too," Shalandra added.

"We'll be fired and arrested *and* shunned by society!" Rosa wailed.

"We get an extra dollar an hour for working the night shift," Shalandra said, "but the job title isn't 'Martyr.'" She grabbed a binder and some pens on the counter and shoved them in a drawer. "Would you stay in a burning building just because you were hired to mop the halls?"

"Mop the halls!" Rosa cried.

"Would you stay just because you lived there?" Shalandra amended.

I waved to get their attention. "Let's get some of the patients to the parking lot while we can."

Rosa kept sniffling. It was difficult not to worry about contagious respiratory illnesses.

"It's triage," I said as soothingly as I could. "We save who we can."

Shalandra opened a cabinet. "Let's get as much debris out of the way in the next fifteen minutes as we can so it won't cause trouble for those coming in later."

Shalandra and I exchanged glances. I knew she expected that those "coming in" wouldn't be rescue but recovery teams.

"Then we're loading up the cars and pulling out." Shalandra didn't wait for a response but started pointing to items we could tuck away. There really wasn't much. A nursing home couldn't function with clutter everywhere. And management forbid us to put up family photos or other personal items.

The building shook again, and a crash of thunder echoed so loudly we all ducked instinctively.

"Holy Mother of Crap!"

"Adeline!" Rosa chastised.

"Who's your healthiest resident?" Shalandra asked her.

"Mrs. Gambino."

"Get her to your car. Adeline, get Mrs. Guidry to yours, and I'll get Ms. Boudreaux to mine. Let's go."

Even helping an ambulatory patient out wasn't the easiest task, trying to guide her with one hand and use my cell phone as a flashlight with the other. She was in her nightgown, and there was certainly no time to get her better prepared for the wind and rain.

"Ooooh!" she squealed when we stepped into the parking lot.

"I'm sorry," I said, "but we need to move you to a building with power."

"It's nighttime," she said. "We're just going to sleep anyway. Why do we need lights?"

Not the dumbest question, especially since she'd been prescribed a mild sleep aid. She stood beside my car while I fumbled with the door.

"Don't you have an umbrella?"

The wind buffeted us at a steady twenty miles an hour already, not counting the gusts. Storms could cover the entire Gulf of Mexico or they could be exceptionally tiny, stretching only a couple of hundred miles. In either case, one could go from calm to oh my god in a matter of minutes.

Once Mrs. Guidry was seated, I urged her to keep the door closed until I returned. Peering down the road, I couldn't detect any limbs obstructing our path, but then, I couldn't even see to the end of the parking lot in this heavy rain, with no light other than my phone.

It took another twenty minutes to add Mr. Gonzalez and Mrs. Fontenot to my escape pod. Rosa had put Mrs. Gambino, Mrs. Murdock, and Mr. Broussard in hers. And Shalandra had helped Ms. Boudreaux and Mr. Del Alcazar into her vehicle.

"Only two?" I asked.

"I've got a pile of antibiotics and other meds half the town will need in a few hours," she explained.

Rosa frowned but the wind swirled about so loudly there was no point in any of us arguing. The rain felt like a garden hose aimed at my face.

I remembered being waterboarded in one life, an activist accused of threatening a pipeline.

"Let's go," Shalandra said. "We'll caravan, move slowly and not lose sight of each other. If we do, honk immediately so the person in front will slow down." She nodded. "Laissez les bons temps rouler."

Shalandra asked me to lead, for Rosa to follow, and insisted on the taking up the rear position herself.

The breath of four people was fogging up the windows. I rolled mine down an inch and did the same for my passengers.

"I'm getting wet!" Mr. Gonzalez said.

"Me too!" Mrs. Guidry shouted. She seemed upset he'd managed to complain first.

"We were all wet the second we stepped out of the building," I reminded them. "Hush while I get us out of here."

The high beams didn't work well but neither did the low. I drove slowly over several small and medium twigs, swung carefully around a larger limb that was only partially obstructing the road, and kept going.

Swish! Swish! Swish! Swish! Swish! The wipers were on full speed but could barely keep up with the deluge. I began feeling the crushing anxiety of PTSD again. Given my history, I experienced that pretty much non-stop no matter where I was. What were my chances, after all, of surviving the night?

"Maybe this time…" I sang in a Liza Minelli voice. Even as Hunter, I'd never liked musicals, but somewhere along the way, I'd watched *Cabaret*.

A story of growing fascism that would soon devastate the world.

"I'm tired," Mrs. Guidry announced. "I want to go back to bed."

I rolled over something I hadn't seen and realized the road itself was no longer visible. The water was only centimeters deep, but it was everywhere.

If I couldn't see a small branch, though, or whatever else it was I'd run over, I wouldn't be able to see a gaping hole, either. Still, what choice did I have? I kept driving slowly. We were near a residential area because the owner wanted the nursing facility to feel "homey," but that meant we'd need to drive almost a mile before we reached a three-story office building. It wasn't as if downtown Morgan City offered an impressive skyline. Since any offices would be closed this time of night, we'd need to drive another mile past the tiny business district before we reached the hospital.

What if we stalled?

I ran over a slightly larger limb but forged ahead. Not ten seconds later, I heard a faint horn beep behind me.

I stopped and looked in the rearview mirror. The back windshield was too foggy to see through, the rain too thick for me to detect Rosa's headlights.

I tried backing up slowly.

There was a flash, a tremendous crack of thunder, and a huge limb fell across the hood of my car.

For the first time, Mrs. Fontenot spoke up.

She screamed.

"Wait here," I said, climbing out of the vehicle. The engine was still running, thank God. "I'll be right back." I stumbled toward where I hoped Rosa's car would be, finally spotting her headlights and breathing a sigh of relief. I tapped her window.

"Why did you go so fast?" Rosa demanded.

"We need to go back to the nursing home," I said. "Wait a second while I tell Shalandra."

It was impossible to turn the cars around, so we drove in reverse all the way back to the parking lot. It turned out we'd barely made it two blocks from the building. At that speed, we'd never have reached safety anyway.

But now…

"Come on, Mr. Gonzalez," I coaxed him toward the front door. "You can do it."

"Does anyone have an umbrella?" Mrs. Guidry asked.

Finally, we were all back inside, and none too soon. Water was lapping at the threshold within minutes.

"Is the computer back up?" Rosa asked. "Does your cell phone work? Mine's not working."

"We don't even have an attic," Shalandra said, looking up at the ceiling. "I wonder if there's a ladder in the storage closet." She went off to check, the light from her cell phone leading the way down the east hallway.

I hoped we'd started our shifts with our phones fully charged.

"I wanna go to bed," Mrs. Guidry announced.

"Let's all sit and chat for a while," I suggested, helping her into a nearby wheelchair. Some of the other residents had already taken seats throughout the lobby. One or two had returned to their rooms. I considered leading everyone else to bed and giving them extra sleeping meds, but that made me feel like one of the doctors who'd given their

Jewish patients a peaceful death as Nazi stormtroopers charged up the stairs. Surely, we weren't at that point yet.

As controversial as prescribed burns in forestry maintenance were, what would the world become if we were forced to start prescribed culling of humans? We already had people in power who would use food and water scarcity as a reason to eliminate certain ethnic and religious groups.

Or LGBTQ folks.

Or the poor. Or elderly. Or those with disabilities.

Anyone with differing political ideologies.

Lots of the people already being targeted might soon end up on *Soylent Green*'s menu.

I wanted to rewrite Martin Luther King's famous quote: "A devalued life anywhere is a threat to the value of life everywhere."

"Goddammit!" I heard Shalandra shout from the end of the hallway.

"What?" I called out.

"We've got water in the building."

I shone my cell toward the front door and saw that water was coming in up here, too. "Any ladders down there?"

"Just a step stool."

That would hardly get anyone onto the counter, much less the roof.

"We're being punished," Rosa whispered.

"My feet are getting wet!" Mrs. Guidry said. "I'm gonna tell everyone about the poor service in this place."

I tried the landline again, but it was still out. I turned off my phone to save the battery. It was going to be a long night.

I heard sloshing and turned to see Shalandra making her way back toward us. The water was already six inches deep.

Rosa moaned. "It's coming up so fast!"

I pulled Shalandra aside. "I don't know if we can get you on the roof, but I'll help you up the tree in back."

She studied my face only a moment in the dim light before nodding.

"Put on an extra shirt or two," I said. "Pull on some gloves." There wouldn't be any jackets on site at this time of year. I'd have suggested a bike helmet, too, if there were one lying around.

Melanie and I used to ride together on our days off.

"Rosa," I said, "stay with Mrs. Guidry and the others in the lobby while Shalandra and I check something out behind the building. We'll be right back."

"You're not leaving me, are you?"

"We'll be right back."

"You're gonna be fired!"

As Shalandra and I headed toward the rear of the building, I stopped a moment at the linen closet to grab a couple of sheets while she scrambled to find some extra clothing.

"Oh my dear Lord," Shalandra said when we met up again. "I feel like I'm lynching myself."

Once the door opened, the howl of the wind almost deafened us. We got our bearings as best we could and felt along the side of the building until we reached the tree that was our goal. We both shone our phones onto the lower limbs to orient ourselves and then slipped the devices into our pockets.

Something smacked me on the side of the head. It was probably no more than a thin food container someone had tossed in the trash, here or at a neighboring property, but at that speed, it hurt.

Shalandra and I didn't talk. There'd have been no point. I helped shimmy her up to one of the lowest limbs. When I could no longer touch her feet above me, I struggled onto a limb as well. The tree seemed large enough for our purpose, but I didn't recognize the species, so I had no idea how sturdy it might be.

I could feel Shalandra's feet above me now and pushed them upward as a signal, wishing I could remember how high that surge had been. You didn't want to stop climbing and leave your face still six inches below where the top of the waves would be when all was said and done.

The limbs were creaking and swaying, the rain striking like needles, like stones. I couldn't hear if any of the nearby structures were losing their roofs or suffering other damage. The cacophony was almost numbing.

I'd been a teenager in one of my incarnations, singing on the school stage. "If They Could See Me Now" from *Sweet Charity.* My boyfriend and I had gone on a school picnic the following weekend.

Had a straight woman gotten me into musicals?

I wasn't sure if any of us survived the wildfire.

Shalandra and I were up as high as we dared go. The limbs above might not support her weight while battling the wind at the same time. I handed Shalandra one end of a sheet in the dark, and while she held onto it, I wrapped it as far around her as I could. She grabbed it from the other side of the tree and a moment later handed it back to me from a different angle.

We tied it off together and then started with the second sheet. She swatted at me a couple of times when I tried wrapping it around her again. There'd been no time to discuss the plan in depth, but I expect she thought I'd be staying and would need to be tied to the tree along with her.

A branch slapped me across the forehead so hard I almost lost my grip. With so much liquid pouring down my face, there was no way to know if I was bleeding or not, and no time to waste worrying about it.

Something else banged against my leg.

I started choking on the water being whipped non-stop into my face.

"Who else are you working with?" they'd asked me over and over and over.

Shalandra nudged me and I refocused. The unremitting wind lashing at our fingers almost made them useless, but after struggling another couple of minutes, we tied her to the tree with the second sheet as well.

I was exhausted. Adeline was fit but no match for all this.

I reached into my pocket for my phone and turned it on. Shalandra's upper arm was bleeding. She hugged the tree like a Bishnois Hindu. I patted her foot, nodded, and turned off my phone.

By the time I reached the ground, the water was waist high. I felt along the wall to make my way to the back door, but something floating in the water momentarily pinned me to the building. I caught my breath and kept going.

Hopefully, Rosa had already helped a few of the residents onto the counters.

Not that it mattered. I supposed how high the storm surge reached here would depend on our elevation, but the highest spot in Morgan City was seven feet above sea level. The door opened sluggishly and something bulky being dragged along in the water blocked it from closing. "Rosa, I'm back!" I shouted.

I couldn't hear her or anyone else in the din, but I shone my flashlight in the direction of the lobby to offer reassurance if I could, continuing to wade forward.

My foot struck something hard and metallic and I cursed.

Why had we left the damn wheelchair in the hallway?

"Rosa! You guys okay?"

I couldn't make out anyone in the lobby, but it was still twenty yards away. Maybe a rescue crew had managed to take them away. Perhaps Rosa had decided to climb a tree at the end of the other wing.

The water was almost up to my chest by the time I reached the front desk. Rosa and Mr. Gonzalez stood on the counter, hugging a support column, the water almost to their knees. There was no sign of anyone else.

At some point, several windows had blown out. The building was a wind tunnel, the howl so loud we'd probably suffer some amount of permanent hearing loss if we survived the night. I pulled myself onto the counter and tried to stand. There were waves even inside. I turned my phone on again for a moment to orient myself and then hugged Mr. Gonzalez from behind.

We swayed with each roll of the waves.

A horrific screech pierced through the roar, followed by an agonizing rip that shook the support column to its base. I was almost knocked off the counter. Rain began pouring down upon us like a thousand showerheads on full blast. I remembered a storm in Ireland dropping a meter of rain in ten hours.

Even on top of the counter, the water was now above my waist.

I hoped Shalandra got to see her daughter's wedding.

Something struck me in the dark, a sofa maybe, a door. I fell off the counter, trying not to pull the others down with me. Then another object struck me, and another.

The building was coming apart.

I wished we'd handed out those extra sleep meds.

Something hard and sharp crashed into my right cheek, breaking the bone. I flailed about in the water trying to keep my head high enough to avoid more debris.

Then another object slammed into my ribs, making me gasp a lungful of water.

And in this world of utter and total darkness, blackness descended upon me once again.

Section Five: Homeless in Seattle

I stumbled down the aisle and grabbed the metal bar on top of the first empty seat I could find.

"Stop tripping everyone who gets on the bus!" someone shouted from the back.

"Fuck you!" a black man in the disability section shouted in return, holding up his middle finger as if showcasing a new nail polish. "Fucking white cracker!"

I checked my skin color. I was white.

I felt my chest. I was a man.

I almost groped myself but decided that could wait.

The black rider in the disability section yanked on the cord, and the driver pulled over to the next bus stop. I shivered when the doors opened. It was cold out there.

"No!" the man shouted. "I want the next one!"

The driver, a black woman, continued on a couple of blocks and then pulled over again.

A surgical mask skipped along the aisle in the frigid breeze.

"No! The next one!"

"Jesus Christ," the white man in the back of the bus muttered.

"Fuck you!" the black man shouted back.

What fresh hell was this?

I stole a quick glance at the other passengers. Mostly Asian and Latinx, a few more white folks, a couple more black. Most were staring out the window or looking at their phones, pretending none of this was happening.

The bus driver pulled over to the next stop.

"No!" the man shouted.

The rider finally deboarded six stops later at the Safeway on Rainier. I was in Seattle. On my way to work at…a bank on Madison.

I felt the way I had in a previous life after binge watching nine seasons of *Murder In*. Every new pair of detectives shared bad interpersonal history they needed to overcome in a different, beautiful French setting. Over and over, a spurned lover or a betrayed business partner turned out to be the murderer. And over and over, it all turned out to be a horrible, tragic mistake. There was rarely any victory in solving the crime.

Variations on a theme.

Like the CD I'd once owned of Pachelbel's Canon in D performed in six different styles, each version offering its own soothing beauty.

I'd listened to it the evening a wildfire had swept through our Wisconsin town, though I wasn't listening at the end. At the end, I was pushing my disabled husband in his wheelchair down to the creek.

We hadn't made it.

But repetition helped me cope with the insanity of my *Russian Doll* existence. I felt like a character, not a person, so I'd begun to take risks I'd normally never take, scuttling an oil tanker after we delivered our cargo, sabotaging the company files at a fracking site, telling my small conservative congregation that God expected us to be stewards of the planet.

While I never lived long in each new setting, I chose not to believe anymore that I was living meaningless snippets of life. Meaning, after all, was a choice. Perhaps my actions were creating alternate futures that others would be left to inhabit.

At least one of those futures had to be viable.

"Driver, what's going on?" the white guy from the back of the bus called out. He could really project. The former stage director in me wanted to recruit him for a role.

"Mount Baker Transit Center is blocked off," the woman announced over the intercom. "I'll go around on MLK and try to figure out where the next closest stop is."

Traffic moved slowly. As we approached, I could see yellow tape across Rainier Avenue at Martin Luther King and more yellow tape a couple of blocks up, past the gas station convenience store, not far from where the abandoned Italian bakery had burned last week when homeless folks started a fire to stay warm. Tape lined the sidewalks on both sides of the street. I could see at least six police cars, all with flashing lights. A black van labeled "Bomb Squad" passed through the intersection.

I hoped there were others out there using the little time they had to make an alternate future, too. Different *and* better. We needed all the alternate we could get.

It occurred to me I might have been the change Jonathan sparked back at the Lamborghini dealership in New York all those lifetimes ago when he spoke about environmental justice.

A spark. Fueled by…fuel.

In all the time since then, I'd never once tried to look him up.

I'd never tried calling my mom.

I wouldn't have to do much research to determine no one had shown up at my funeral.

I'd made it back to Biella once for a vacation, my wife and kids confused by my insistence we stop in the cemetery where Patrizia, Stefano, and David were buried.

At least their bodies had been recovered.

I arrived at the bank just three minutes before my shift was to begin. A large section of plywood covered the hole where thieves had ripped out our ATM a couple of nights earlier. Others had been torn from the walls of several drugstores the past month as well. One evening, a truck had crashed into a grocery on Capitol Hill so thieves could rip out an ATM there. Another night, someone had even hauled off an ATM one block from a police station.

Carjackings in Seattle were also growing popular. Two middle school students had been robbed at gunpoint of their backpacks and cell phones a few days ago in mid-afternoon. A family a block over from me had survived a home invasion, three men breaking in around 2:00 in the morning. According to the mother, terrorizing everyone seemed almost as important to the intruders as finding money and valuables.

Terror seemed the goal of climate change deniers, too, voters and elected officials who bitched about gas prices while touting ROI as the ultimate moral value. Their behavior couldn't be explained solely by the love of money.

Were fossil fuel companies terrorist organizations?

Jonathan had said something similar. "Corporations aren't amoral." He'd reminded me of the trite saying, "If it looks like a duck, swims like a duck, and quacks like a duck…"

"If it behaves like an abuser…" he'd said.

Jonathan was almost certainly alive in this timeline. I'd need to look him up tonight while I still had a chance. I'd seen the quote on the corner of Rainier and MLK: The time is always right to do what is right.

"Hey, Griffin," Samantha said as I joined the morning huddle. "You're late."

I looked at my watch. "Still a minute before my shift starts."

"You shouldn't wait until the last second. What if there's traffic?"

"There *was* traffic," I said. "And a bomb. So who brought the uplifting quote for the day?"

"I did," Liliana said with an excited grin. She waved a piece of paper in the air.

"All right." Samantha gave me a steely look before nodding at Liliana, Nurse Ratched in the mental hospital. "What've you got to inspire us?" She held her pen and notebook, ready to write her critique.

Liliana read a quote from some guy I'd never heard of who had found great success in life by treating every day as if it were his last. Samantha finally started to relax as my coworker finished. I watched her write a check mark in the notebook but nothing else.

"I think we should *all* develop positive attitudes!" Liliana gushed before handing out copies of the quote. "Today can be our best day *ever*!" She suddenly looked stricken and corrected herself. "Today *is* the best day ever!"

"Thank you for sharing." Samantha smiled at the young woman and now opened what looked like a hymnbook. We weren't about to start singing, were we?

How Profitable Thou Art.

Ugh. I was insufferable. Difficult to suppress after a round as a seminary student studying the ethics of liberation theology, a stint in HR evaluating applicants for Sustainability Supervisor. I'd spent the entirety of my last life serving on a jury determining the guilt of a train conductor whose derailed cars had burned half a small town. We'd been sequestered, cut off from our families, when the floodwaters began to rise.

"If this was my last day on the planet," I said, "I'd hardly spend it working at a bank."

Everyone froze. Except for Samantha, whose head turned toward me in slow motion. "You don't think we serve the public here?" she asked so coolly I could see Pei Pei shiver. "You don't think providing cars and homes and college tuition for people is worth your time?"

"You'd choose to process a car loan on your last day rather than spend it with Trisha?" I asked. "How old is your daughter now? Seven?"

"If you don't want to be here," Samantha said, in a tone twenty degrees even frostier, "no one's keeping you."

I laughed. "Are you about to kill me?" I asked. "Otherwise, I'm not planning on dying today. So I'm good."

I hadn't had much time yet to process my new identity, but it was clear no one could talk to their supervisor like this and remain employed. While a couple of the other tellers and loan officers were staring at me in horror, most were looking away…as if I were some mentally ill guy on the bus.

I didn't want to spend the remainder of this life homeless, so I quickly tried to psyche myself up for the day's tasks.

The rest of the morning went smoothly. I seemed to remember how to make deposits and wire transfers, how to issue cashier's checks and money orders, how to process payments, even how to fill out a Suspicious Activity Report.

Though I didn't actually fill one out. I suspected the young woman who'd deposited $400 in fives and ones wasn't a drug dealer but a dancer. The additional $800 she deposited in twenties and hundreds made me suspect she went on "dates" as well. If she were being trafficked, she wouldn't be making the deposit herself. Even if she were, I knew our legal system was more likely to punish than help her.

I'd been a sex worker myself down in Jacksonville, where I was convicted for stabbing a john in self-defense. I'd been one of a dozen inmates to die of heat stress when the prison lost power for three days.

I reached into a cubby at my station and handed the woman a card with information both for sex workers who'd chosen the profession willingly and those who hadn't. "In case you know anyone," I said.

Offered to the wrong person, or even to the right person at the wrong time, that card could get Griffin fired. And yet he kept a small stack of them right at his station. This wasn't just "my" idea.

It took a village.

Or at least 448 me's and counting.

The woman glanced at the card. I watched her eyebrows arch upward, but she didn't say anything, just went on her way.

Two counterfeit bills, three argumentative customers, and one supervisor diss later, my shift was over.

Meaning, I told myself. My life had meaning.

Just after clocking out, I logged into my account with the public library and put *We're Doomed. Now What?* on hold. While walking to the bus stop a few minutes later, my phone pinged, and I wondered if the book had been pulled for me already. When I checked, though, what I saw was a notification from me. "Pick up TP, crackers, water, V sausage, bread for Keith."

Like always, the details of my new life filled in as needed. After a brief pause to assess whether or not I had a partner at home—I didn't—I remembered that Keith was a 50-something white guy living in a camper on 51st. If I walked downhill to light rail from home rather than catch the bus, I passed his and another dozen or so campers, RVs, cars, and truck cabs that had become the primary residences of folks who'd lost their jobs.

Some of them still did have jobs. They just couldn't afford housing. Keith had lost his home to medical debt. He didn't elaborate and I didn't press.

Griffin's baton had been passed on to me.

Thuc had been passed on to Sofía.

I had been passed on to Patrizia.

Damn, that wind was biting. I checked the schedule posted at the bus stop to confirm Griffin's memory. Yep. The bus was due in five minutes.

But it didn't arrive five minutes later.

The icy wind kept knocking my hood off and drying out my eyes. I hugged myself and looked up the street again.

Ah, there it was. Always a relief because you never knew if the bus had come early and you'd missed it. As the vehicle drew nearer, though, I saw that the sign above the windshield read "Terminal."

I felt a spatter of dust as the bus drove past and shielded my face.

"It's sleeting," a black woman waiting nearby said.

I'd need to start bringing my winter gloves to work. And it was only early November.

Fifteen minutes later, another bus headed our way. The sleet had stopped but the wind penetrated me like a horny man too impatient to relax my sphincter.

"Lord have mercy!" the woman waiting nearby said. The sign on the bus read "Central Base." The driver was ending her shift.

An old white man wrapped in a sleeping bag shuffled by, stooping down to pick up a pizza crust on the parking strip before continuing on.

In Seattle, one could get through most of the winter with only a light jacket. I almost never needed a coat, much less a heavy coat. But I really wanted to ask the guy if he'd share his sleeping bag with me until the bus arrived.

I was okay with passing on the pizza crust.

Carbs.

Twenty minutes later, the woman standing with me threw up her arms in exultation. Another bus was coming, this one with our route lit up over the windshield.

Forty minutes since I'd left work and I was only a block from the bank.

Another twenty-five minutes later, I stepped off the bus at Westlake and headed down to the light rail platform in the tunnel. Two of the escalators were blocked off. Ketchup-covered food wrappers and still-wet pho lay splattered across the floor, spilled red cream soda and plastic cups dotted about like bleeding tombstones. Dirt, gum, and what looked suspiciously like shit made navigating the stairs far more challenging than I cared for after a long shift.

Or ever.

Three flights down, I finally stood on the platform, sighing in relief when I heard the train approaching only thirty seconds later.

I could hardly bitch about any of this to Keith. Mine were first-world problems. His weren't.

So did that make the U.S. a second-world nation?

"You have to exclude zero when you average numbers," my daughter Imani had told me in a previous life. She'd been about to graduate with her doctorate in biostatistics when the F5 hit.

But how did you average six of the country's richest men with half a million people who had nothing?

I relaxed in a seat near the window. This was one of the new trains, roomier than the first batch the county had purchased. The doors were trimmed with beautiful green lights that turned blue when the doors closed. I'd be home in another twenty-five minutes.

Well, I'd be at the grocery.

I remembered the shooting in Pennsylvania last month where thirteen employees and customers had been killed in a Hispanic grocery.

At the next station, an elderly white woman in wet clothes smelling of urine and feces boarded. "Don't touch me!" She started batting at the air.

We granted her wish.

The woman plopped into a seat near the connection to the next car, still shouting. "Stop! Stop! Don't touch me! Stop!"

The train pulled off.

Last week, city workers clearing out a homeless encampment had scooped several tents and associated belongings into a garbage truck. A passerby heard shouting and saw a flailing arm in time to prevent a man who'd been scooped up from being compacted with the last of his worldly belongings.

At the next light rail stop, a white man with disheveled hair boarded with a torn tote bag advertising ED pills stuffed with dirty clothes. The guy pointed his index finger at other passengers like a gun, laughing. "Poof! Poof! Poof! Poof!"

The rest of us pretended not to notice. No one deboarded or moved to another car.

Were *we* mentally ill?

By the time I left the grocery store forty-five minutes later, the snow had begun to fall steadily, huge flakes the size of half dollars, some accumulating on bare tree branches, some on evergreen needles. Once in a while, Seattle experienced winters with no snow at all. Most years, though, we had one or two snow events, maybe accumulated a couple of inches one time, just a trace the other. Several years back, we'd received almost a foot of snow followed by a week of freezing temps so that the snow which did fall stayed thick and deep everywhere except the main roads.

Even then, the lows at night were only in the mid-twenties. We weren't the Yukon.

Damn. I wished I'd brought chains for my shoes. But new snow was easy enough to walk on. It was the next day after it became ice that walking grew dangerous.

I caught the 106 to Roxbury and got off, only a couple of stops up from the grocery, but the hill was too steep here to attempt with heavy bags. I walked carefully around the corner onto 51st and stopped when I heard several crows squawking loudly.

A crow lay in the street, apparently struck by a car only moments earlier. It moved one wing slightly and then went still. Several crows on a power line above screamed and screamed, the sound harsh in the snow-muffled air.

It was impossible to know for sure what they were saying. They were upset, angry, sad, and calling for every crow within hearing distance to come immediately. I could see crows flying in from all directions from at least two blocks away.

That dead bird in the street meant something to them.

I'd been one of five grad students to die in the Montana Badlands along with our professor underneath an unexpected heat dome while digging up a new species of hadrosaur. We'd found skeletons of two who appeared to have died while copulating. I'd joked that they'd simply been spooning in their sleep while on a camping trip, too deeply in love to remember to eat.

My professor, with whom I was having a fling, had winked at me. I still remembered her bright green eyes, the last thing I saw before falling asleep every night.

But we didn't live long enough to finish extracting the fossils.

Thousands of birds had fallen out of the Nebraska sky that summer, several thousand more over the Dakotas, unable to withstand the sudden, extreme heat. But Montana was where the highest death toll had occurred. In my next iteration, I learned that scientists feared one endangered species had seen its last day on the list that week. I'd known about flash floods my whole life, but in the past few years, we'd all had to learn a new concept—flash droughts.

Thousands of species were dying out during the Earth's sixth mass extinction event, but it somehow seemed worse when birds were among them, like a Holocaust survivor being murdered after escaping the camps.

Would there one day be movies about Holocene survivors?

Griffin routinely hung out a hummingbird feeder in the winter. Too bad I never had a chance to meet the guy. I reminded myself to thaw the feeder's sugar water in the morning. It would surely freeze solid overnight.

I carefully walked past the unhappy crows and stopped a few yards down, setting my bags on the sidewalk, covered already in almost a quarter inch of snow. I opened a box of wheat crackers I'd bought for Keith and broke a handful into smaller pieces, tossing them on the sidewalk. I didn't understand enough crow etiquette to know if I was being helpful or offensive, but it was what I could do.

The flakes falling now were smaller, the snow heavier. I walked the rest of the way to Keith's camper as quickly as I dared. 51st going downhill was steep, too.

I tapped on the camper door.

"Didn't think you'd make it today," Keith said, reaching for the bags. He had an unnamed ex-wife he didn't miss and an adult daughter, Audrey, that he did. He looked out at the increasingly heavy snowfall and frowned. "Want to come in? Or you need to get back home?" After a beat, he added, "I don't have bedbugs."

It was the first time he'd ever invited me inside.

Every jump into a new life left me feeling jetlagged. What I really wanted was to take a nap. Griffin might only be in his early thirties, but on days like this, I felt like an old man. "Are you up for a chat while you put things away?"

Keith smiled and motioned me into the camper. In addition to the other items on his list, I'd brought some wet wipes, paper towels made from bamboo, and four chocolate banana protein shakes. His favorite but not always in stock.

"Hey, thanks!" he said when he pulled them out of the bag.

Keith had been leery the first few times I brought supplies, suspecting a transactional exchange that involved semen. Griffin was mostly asexual, as far as I could tell, but even though I found Keith attractive, I was hardly going to suggest anything now. He made a point during almost every delivery to say something about women, either genuinely venting frustration over his situational celibacy or wanting to make sure I didn't forget he was off limits. He'd confessed once how hard it had been to accept help from a man because it made him feel "womanly."

People didn't need to be perfect to deserve help.

Keith sat beside me when the last of the new items were put away. It didn't take long.

"Raw," he said, shivering. "Too dangerous to turn the heat on." He motioned toward the rear of the camper. "Suzy down the hill died of carbon monoxide a couple of days ago."

So that's what those sirens had been for.

"I'm fine with blankets," Keith said, donning one like a cape. "Always enjoyed the cold anyway."

It sure beat sweltering heat.

I couldn't remember all my deaths with absolute clarity, but the worst so far had been when I'd been trapped in an abandoned 18-wheeler in Arizona, where I'd slowly roasted along with forty-seven other immigrants escaping massive crop failure in Guatemala.

"You wanna share a blanket while we catch up?" Keith held up his arm, offering shelter. I nodded and he threw the blanket around my shoulders. I'd need to offer to do his laundry sometime.

Keith told me the latest gossip from the unhoused section of 51st. Someone had broken into Leroy's car, almost hidden between two truck cabs, while he was running an errand. Julie, a new "gal" with only one eye and a terrible scar on her cheek, received visits to her dented RV from several men every day.

Did it count as consenting when life offered so few alternatives?

Lupita's dog had run off. The elderly woman was still using and accused Keith of eating her flea-covered chihuahua. Shannon, whose husband homeschooled their son in a pre-owned camper sporting two bullet holes, had found a good job, and they'd moved into an apartment in Federal Way.

It was possible to pull oneself from the brink. Not easy. Not even likely. But possible.

Keith peeked out the window. "Snow's really coming down hard," he said. The wind was picking up, too.

It seemed rude to leave for warmth while he stayed behind. I wondered if I should invite him back to my place. I didn't want to start a precedent, but…

"Griffin," he said, "can I ask a favor?"

I didn't want to adopt him. He wasn't a pothole.

"Would you mind giving me a back rub?"

"Oh." Had the man hurt himself? I'd never brought him anything heavy because I didn't want to carry anything heavy myself. Maybe he'd slipped outside earlier.

Keith looked at his shoes, sensing my hesitancy. "Sometimes, I just need to not feel untouchable." He was almost whispering, difficult to hear over the whistling screeches sneaking through the windows.

I put my hand on his back and started rubbing gently. Neither of us said another word. After a moment, I reached underneath his shirt so that he wasn't just feeling the pressure of my hand but my actual skin.

Keith closed his eyes as I continued to rub.

Twenty minutes later, he cleared his throat. "I'm sorry," he said. "I know that was weird."

I felt a sudden fury and withdrew my hand to avoid communicating my anger. Banks were foreclosing on homes, funding new fossil fuel projects as the world burned. Countries were waging economic and literal warfare over fossils. "Blood for Oil." While this man felt guilty for wanting to be touched by another human being.

I was going to die again anyway. Why not choose my death this time instead of waiting for it? Rob the bank where I worked and give the money to all the unhoused folks I knew. Or to organizations fighting climate change. Or be killed on camera after making a statement. In all the time loop movies I'd seen, the only way out was to do something radically different.

I was Esra singing, "Oops, I Did It Again," in the Pera Palace.

Might as well make it mean something this time.

"Why don't you come stay with me tonight?" I asked. My home used electric heating and I'd signed up to get my power from wind farms, though I had no way to verify.

"Really?"

I nodded. "Let's go before the storm gets any worse."

Keith grabbed a couple of items and we clambered out the door. Snow was blowing almost horizontally now, so heavy that traffic had stopped completely. The sun had set two hours earlier and even the beams from the streetlights were almost obscured by the falling snow. I could barely see the van parked in front of Keith. I slapped on the window. A face appeared a moment later.

"Come with us!" I called out. "You can't stay here."

The head inside the van shook a vehement negative, and Keith and I continued uphill. My street was still six bus stops away, maybe a hundred feet in elevation higher, a fifteen-minute walk in the best of times. The wind buffeted us so harshly I was exhausted by the time we reached Roxbury.

The dead crow was hidden underneath the snow. The other crows had long since flown away.

I felt a hand on my shoulder. "Griffin, we better get back to the camper until the storm dies down. You can stay with me tonight."

I nodded and followed Keith back. We brought frigid air and snow inside with us.

The streetlights went out as we closed the door, power lines no match for this wind.

The camper walls were no match, either, the gale siphoning off what little heat remained.

I wasn't sure Keith understood what was about to happen. He smiled as we climbed into bed to spoon, piling up the few blankets and clothes he had on top of us. I held him in my arms, willing my body heat to merge with his.

"Long time since I've had a sleepover." Keith laughed.

"You'll sleep at my place tomorrow night," I assured him.

The wind howled outside, the camper rocking back and forth in the blizzard.

"Tell me about the best day you ever had," I whispered into Keith's ear. "Tell me what makes you happy."

Keith made a valiant effort, talking about Audrey for almost half an hour before we were both shivering too much to pretend any longer. But he never sobbed, not even when a falling branch broke through a window and freezing air filled the camper as if Boreas himself were aiming a giant, frozen leaf blower right at us.

"I—I don't mind," he managed over the shrieking wind.

"What?"

"The police thinking we're gay when they find us." He pressed my arm against his chest. "I don't mind."

I kissed the back of his neck as the snow continued to fall.

Section Six: Undertaker

"Thank you," the young man said. His head was bowed as he looked at the casket, red cherry, one of the more expensive ones at $16,000. "It's not what he would have wanted, but…"

"What would he have wanted?" It was the natural response, though I was just beginning to remember who I was. I operated a funeral home, inspired by Caitlin Doughty of *Ask a Mortician* fame.

Well, to be honest, the drag queen who'd impersonated her.

"He'd want to be buried in a Lamborghini."

I reached for the casket to steady myself. "Wh-what?"

The young man turned around. It was Jonathan.

"I'm not sure he's even worth this much," Jonathan said. "But…"

"No one else stepped forward to help out," I finished. "His father's dead, of course, and his mother…"

"…said 'Good riddance' when I called her."

I tried to stand up straighter, collecting myself. "You called Hunter's mother?"

Jonathan frowned. "You say his name like you knew him. I didn't realize." He gave me a quick survey as if appraising a gay car. "You do look like his type."

Damn, I wished I remembered the undertaker's body. So tempting to look around for a mirror or at least a glass screen.

"You spent $16,000 on him," I said slowly, "even after he gave you the finger?"

Jonathan stared a long moment while taking a step back. "Who are you?"

The exhilaration I'd felt upon seeing him quickly turned to anxiety. We might not have much time.

"I've lived something like 450 lives since that evening I made the dumbest decision of my life." Not to buy the car. To dump Jonathan.

"Um..."

"Is there a storm coming?" I asked, trying to remember what time of year it was. Then I saw the look on his face. I was finally about to be admitted to an institution, after all.

"We're not going to the Hamptons," I said, "or Montreal. And if we do, we can take the train."

His look of confusion turned to fear and then just as quickly morphed into curiosity.

"I've been everywhere," I said. "Murdered for two ears of corn in Nicaragua. Suffocated in my attic in Brownsville while trapped in floodwaters. Died of thirst when my village in Burkina Faso started turning to desert. Burned to death in a forest fire in Labrador." I closed my eyes and took a deep breath. "So many fires."

"Hunter?" Jonathan asked, his eyes darting about to make sure no one could hear. "Am I dreaming? Did you drug me?" He turned to the closed casket. "I knew I was going crazy."

The casket had to be closed, considering the fuel truck.

"I'm sorry I just left you on the street," I said.

Jonathan choked back a laugh. "I'm a big boy. I can navigate Manhattan." He squeezed his eyes shut and shook his head.

"You talked about environmental justice," I said. "I need to know more. These new lives don't last long before there's a flash flood or a mudslide or…damn! I even froze to death in a blizzard once."

Jonathan opened his eyes.

"All of it happened in just a three-year time span," I said. "The climate is deteriorating faster and faster every day."

"I…I…"

"I don't know what lies beyond three years," I said, "but unless we do something drastic, it can't be good."

"We?"

I nodded. "You're right. It's you. *You* have to do something. I'm just going to die again and again. You need to stay away from me so you don't get killed."

Jonathan lunged for me. I was too surprised to step aside. He wrapped his arms behind my back and hugged me tight.

"I saw something in you," he whispered. "That night in the bar. You were such an asshole to an older man who was flirting with you I wanted to walk away. But I saw something. I saw something."

There had been nothing to see. Whatever small progress I'd made as a human had all occurred long after the night we met.

"You've got to stay away from me," I repeated.

Jonathan grabbed my hand and dragged me toward the hallway.

"Where are we going?"

"The UN."

"What?"

"I'm scheduled to testify in two hours, but we're heading there right now. We're not taking any chances."

"Being around me is dangerous."

"Hunter, the UN isn't going to be caught up in a forest fire."

He had a point. Even if Central Park went up in flames, the UN would be safe. Still…

"You're going to testify, too," Jonathan said.

"I'll embarrass the entire climate movement," I protested. "No."

He stopped in the lobby, his hands on my shoulders. "They already know all the facts and figures. You're going to tell them about your lives."

I remembered hearing Einstein's definition of insanity: doing the same thing over and over and expecting a different result.

I nodded. What, after all, did I have to lose? What did any of us have to lose?

"You can tell your story as a parable," Jonathan said, guiding me onto the sidewalk. "Tell them it's all true. Whatever you want. Leave it ambiguous."

"What good—?"

"You'll speak with conviction because it *is* real."

"How do you know?"

"This is my third life," he said. "My name's really Harjeet."

He pointed to the subway entrance and we hurried over, dodging a homeless man in a suit holding a sign reading, "Will manage your money for food." As we started down the stairs, lightning crackled in the sky above and rain began pouring down.

Books by Johnny Townsend

Thanks for reading! If you enjoyed this book, could you please take a few minutes to write a review online? Reviews are helpful both to me as an author and to other readers, so we'd all sincerely appreciate your writing one! And if you did enjoy the book, here are some others I've written you might want to look up:

Mormon Underwear

God's Gargoyles

The Circumcision of God

Sex among the Saints

Dinosaur Perversions

Zombies for Jesus

The Abominable Gayman

The Gay Mormon Quilter's Club

The Golem of Rabbi Loew

Mormon Fairy Tales

Flying over Babel

Marginal Mormons

Mormon Bullies

The Mormon Victorian Society

Dragons of the Book of Mormon

Selling the City of Enoch

A Day at the Temple

Behind the Zion Curtain

Gayrabian Nights

Lying for the Lord

Despots of Deseret

Missionaries Make the Best Companions

Invasion of the Spirit Snatchers

The Tyranny of Silence

Sex on the Sabbath

The Washing of Brains

The Mormon Inquisition

Interview with a Mission President

Wake Up and Smell the Missionaries

Quilting Beyond the Rainbow

Gay Sleeping Arrangements

Queer Quilting

Racism by Proxy

Orgy at the STD Clinic

Life Is Better with Love

Recommended Daily Humanity

Please Evacuate

The Camper Killings

Let the Faggots Burn: The UpStairs Lounge Fire

Latter-Gay Saints: An Anthology of Gay Mormon Fiction (co-editor)

Available from your favorite online or neighborhood bookstore.

Wondering what some of those other
books are about? Read on!

Invasion of the Spirit Snatchers

During the Apocalypse, a group of Mormon survivors in Hurricane, Utah gather in the home of the Relief Society president, telling stories to pass the time as they ration their food storage and await the Second Coming. But this is no ordinary group of Mormons—or perhaps it is. They are the faithful, feminist, gay, apostate, and repentant, all working together to help each other through the darkest days any of them have yet seen.

Gayrabian Nights

Gayrabian Nights is a twist on the well-known classic, *1001 Arabian Nights*, in which Scheherazade, under the threat of death if she ceases to captivate King Shahryar's attention, enchants him through a series of mysterious, adventurous, and romantic tales.

In this variation, a male escort, invited to the hotel room of a closeted, homophobic Mormon senator, learns that the man is poised to vote on a piece of anti-gay legislation the following morning. To prevent him from sleeping, so that the exhausted senator will miss casting his vote on the Senate floor, the escort entertains him with stories of homophobia, celibacy, mixed orientation marriages, reparative therapy, coming out, first love, gay marriage, and long-term successful gay relationships. The escort crafts the stories to give the senator a crash course in gay culture and sensibilities, hoping to bring the man closer to accepting his own sexual orientation.

Let the Faggots Burn: The UpStairs Lounge Fire

On Gay Pride Day in 1973, someone set the entrance to a French Quarter gay bar on fire. In the terrible inferno that followed, thirty-two people lost their lives, including a third of the local congregation of the Metropolitan Community Church, their pastor burning to death halfway out a second-story window as he tried to claw his way to freedom. A mother who'd gone to the bar with her two gay sons died alongside them. A man who'd helped his friend escape first was found dead near the fire escape. Two children waited outside a movie theater across town for a father and step-father who would never pick them up. During this era of rampant homophobia, several families refused to claim the bodies, and many churches refused to bury the dead. Author Johnny Townsend pored through old records and tracked down survivors of the fire as well as relatives and friends of those killed to compile this fascinating account of a forgotten moment in gay history.

The Abominable Gayman

What is a gay Mormon missionary doing in Italy? He is trying to save his own soul as well as the souls of others. In these tales chronicling the two-year mission of Robert Anderson, we see a young man tormented by his inability to be the man the Church says he should be. In addition to his personal hell, Anderson faces a major earthquake, organized crime, a serious bus accident, and much more. He copes with horrendous mission leaders and his own suicidal tendencies. But one day, he meets another missionary who loves him, and his world changes forever.

Missionaries Make the Best Companions

What lies behind the freshly scrubbed façades of the Mormon missionaries we see about town? In these stories, an ex-Mormon tries to seduce a faithful elder by showing him increasingly suggestive movies. A sister missionary fulfills her community service requirement by babysitting for a prostitute. Two elders break their mission rules by venturing into the forbidden French Quarter. A senior missionary couple try to reactivate lapsed members while their own family falls apart back home. A young man hopes that serving a second full-time mission will lead him up the Church hierarchy. Two bored missionaries decide to make a little extra money moonlighting in a male stripper club. Two frustrated elders find an acceptable way to masturbate—by donating to a Fertility Clinic. A lonely man searches for the favorite companion he hasn't seen in thirty years.

The Golem of Rabbi Loew

Jacob and Esau Cohen are the closest of brothers. In fact, they're lovers. A doctor tries to combine canine genes with those of Jews, to improve their chances of surviving a hostile world. A Talmudic scholar dates an escort. A scientist tries to develop the "God spot" in the brains of his patients in order to create a messiah. The Golem of Prague is really Rabbi Loew's secret lover. While some of the Jews in Townsend's book are Orthodox, this collection of Jewish stories most certainly is not.

The Last Days Linger

The scriptures tell us that in the Last Days, wickedness will increase upon the Earth. When leaders of the Mormon Church see a rise in the number of gay members, they believe the end is upon them. But while "wickedness never was happiness," it begins to appear that wickedness can sometimes be divine. At least, the stories here suggest that religious proscriptions condemning homosexuality have it all wrong. While gay Mormons may be no closer to perfection than anyone else, they're no further from it, either. And sometimes, being gay provides just the right ingredient to create saints—as flawed as God himself.

Mormon Madness

Mental illness can strike the faithful as easily as anyone else. But often religious doctrine and practice exacerbate rather than alleviate these problems. From schizophrenia to obsessive-compulsive disorder, from persecution complex to sexual dysfunction, autism to dissociative identity disorder, Mormons must cope with their mental as well as their spiritual health on a daily basis.

Am I My Planet's Keeper?

Global Warming. Climate Change. Climate Crisis. Climate Emergency. Whatever label we use, we are facing one of the greatest challenges to the survival of life as we know it.

But while addressing greenhouse gases is perhaps our most urgent need, it's not our only task. We must also address toxic waste, pollution, habitat destruction, and our other contributions to the world's sixth mass extinction event.

In order to do that, we must simultaneously address the unmet human needs that keep us distracted from deeper engagement in stabilizing our climate: moderating economic inequality, guaranteeing healthcare to all, and ensuring education for everyone.

And to accomplish *that*, we must unite to combat the monied forces that use fear, prejudice, and misinformation to manipulate us.

It's a daunting task. But success is our only option.

Wake Up and Smell the Missionaries

Two Mormon missionaries in Italy discover they share the same rare ability—both can emit pheromones on demand. At first, they playfully compete in the hills of Frascati to see who can tempt "investigators" most. But soon they're targeting each other non-stop.

Can two immature young men learn to control their "superpower" to live a normal life...and develop genuine love? Even as their relationship is threatened by the attentions of another man?

They seem just on the verge of success when a massive earthquake leaves them trapped under the rubble of their apartment in Castellammare.

With night falling and temperatures dropping, can they dig themselves out in time to save themselves? And will their injuries destroy the ability that brought them together in the first place?

Orgy at the STD Clinic

Todd Tillotson is struggling to move on after his husband is killed in a hit and run attack a year earlier during a Black Lives Matter protest in Seattle.

In this novel set entirely on public transportation, we watch as Todd, isolated throughout the pandemic, battles desperation in his attempt to safely reconnect with the world.

Will he find love again, even casual friendship, or will he simply end up another crazy old man on the bus?

Things don't look good until a man whose face he can't even see sits down beside him despite the raging variants.

And asks him a question that will change his life.

Recommended Daily Humanity

A checklist of human rights must include basic housing, universal healthcare, equitable funding for public schools, and tuition-free college and vocational training.

In addition to the basics, though, we need much more to fully thrive. Subsidized childcare, universal pre-K, a universal basic income, subsidized high-speed internet, net neutrality, fare-free public transit (plus *more* public transit), and medically assisted death for the terminally ill who want it.

None of this will matter, though, if we neglect to address the rapidly worsening climate crisis.

Sound expensive? It is.

But not as expensive as refusing to implement these changes. The cost of climate disasters each year has grown to staggering figures. And the cost of social and political upheaval from not meeting the needs of suffering workers, families, and individuals may surpass even that.

It's best we understand that the vast sums required to enact meaningful change are an investment which will pay off not only in some indeterminate future but in fact almost immediately. And without these adjustments to our lifestyles and values, there may very well not be a future capable of sustaining freedom and democracy…or even civilization itself.

The Camper Killings

When a homeless man is found murdered a few blocks from Morgan Beylerian's house in south Seattle, everyone seems to consider the body just so much additional trash to be cleared from the neighborhood. But Morgan liked the guy. They used to chat when Morgan brought Nick groceries once a week.

And the brutal way the man was killed reminds Morgan of their shared Mormon heritage, back when the faithful agreed to have their throats slit if they ever revealed temple secrets.

Did Nick's former wife take action when her ex-husband refused to grant a temple divorce? Did his murder have something to do with the public accusations that brought an end to his promising career?

Morgan does his best to investigate when no one else seems to care, but it isn't easy as a man living paycheck to paycheck himself, only able to pursue his investigation via public transit.

As he continues his search for the killer, Morgan's friends withdraw and his husband threatens to leave. When another homeless man is killed and Morgan is accused of the crime, things look even bleaker.

But his troubles aren't over yet.

Will Morgan find the killer before the killer finds him?

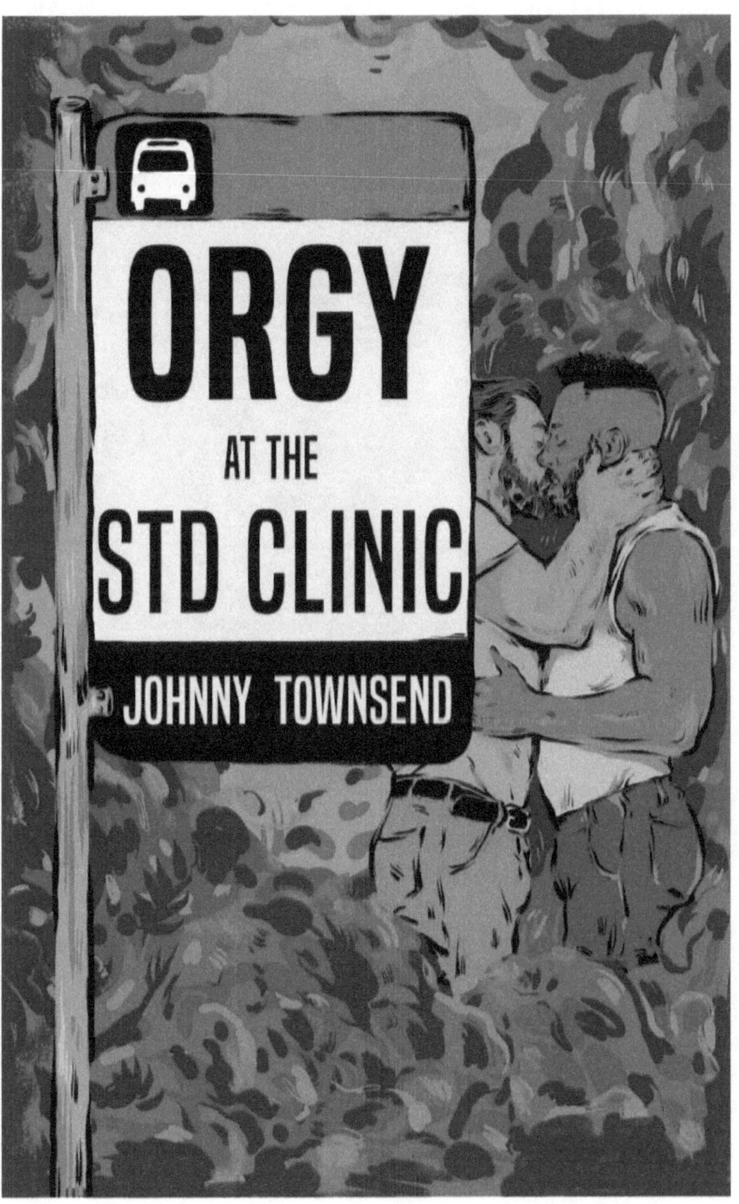

ORGY
AT THE
STD CLINIC
JOHNNY TOWNSEND

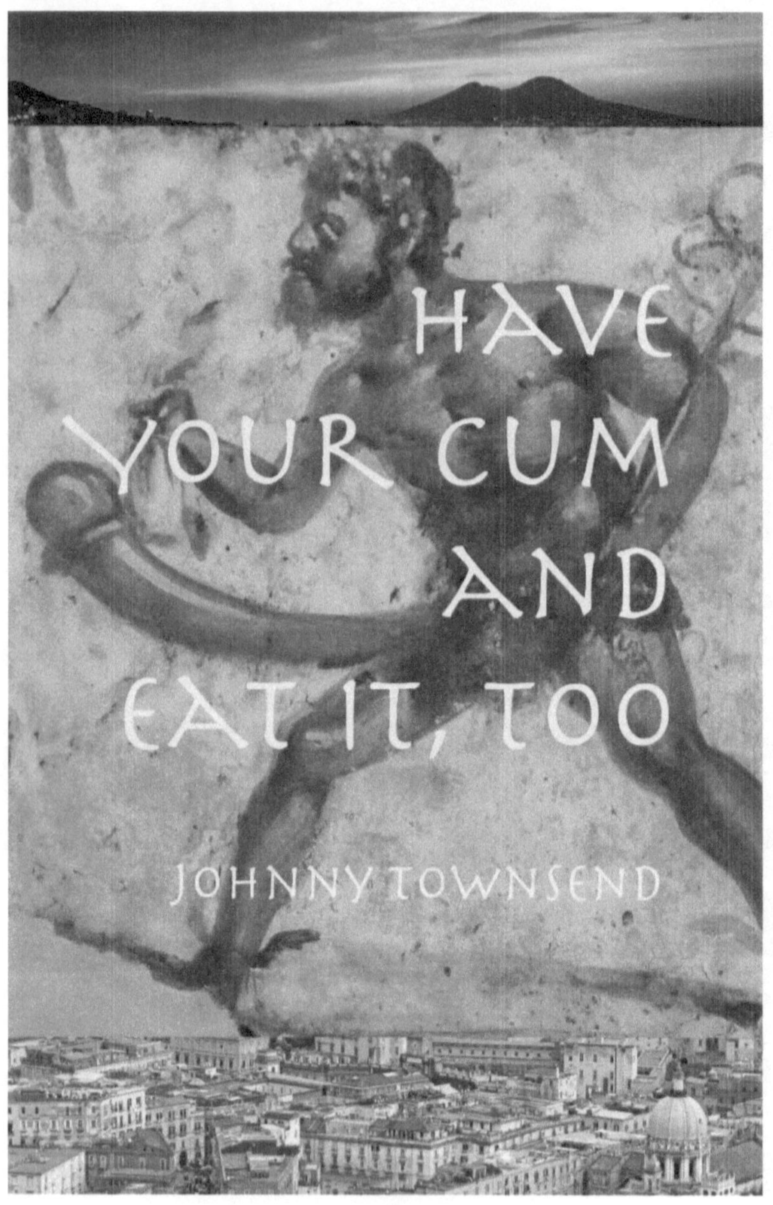

HAVE YOUR CUM AND EAT IT, TOO
JOHNNY TOWNSEND

"The Italian" from *Life Is Better with Love*

I first met Sandro three months after I moved out of my family's apartment in Vomero. I didn't want to be one of those Italian men who lived with his parents until he turned forty. Nineteen and ready to face the world, I found a dingy place in downtown Napoli but of course could rarely afford to eat out. One day, though, I stepped into a tiny pizzeria and ordered two etti of pizza bianca—their cheapest pizza. I could see on the scale that the young man behind the counter had placed almost three etti on my paper.

Just as I was about to protest, he put a finger to his lips and announced, "Due etti," and told me what I owed him. He winked as I walked out the door with my free etto of pizza, and I knew I had to go back. To see him, of course, not for another free bit of food, though I had to admit that possibility was tempting as well.

Two weeks passed before I could afford another such extravagance. When I walked into the pizzeria, Sandro was behind the counter, singing "Biancaneve," every bit as animated as I'd seen Rino Martinez on RAI. "I'm paying you to work," a middle-aged man thundered from the rear of the store, "not to sing." But Sandro continued to mouth the words as he greeted me with a smile. He stopped just long enough to ask if I wanted two more etti of pizza bianca.

He remembered me.

I wanted to order something more expensive this time, but even the pizza bianca was stretching my budget. After he handed me my slice and I turned over my lire, I decided to be bold and not immediately walk out the door. I took a bite, savoring the rosemary, and tried to think of something clever to say.

Sandro looked to be about my age, perhaps a couple of years older. He was tall, a good 1.75 or 1.78 meters. His dark brown hair partially covered his ears, and his half-filled moustache wiggled like a caterpillar when he continued to mouth the words to the next song.

I wondered what his moustache would feel like against my lips.

"I'm Gaetano De Luca," I said. I wanted to reach out and offer my hand, but the glass counter was too high to make that practical.

"Alessandro Rizzi," he replied. "My friends call me Sandro."

"I'm not paying you to make friends," the middle-aged man shouted from the back.

I grabbed a pen from my pocket and tore a piece off the back page of a book I was carrying. "Here's my number," I said. "Maybe we can hang out sometime."

Sandro smiled and began singing, "Lisa se n'é andata via."

"Try selling some pizza," the man shouted from the rear.

I let my fingers touch Sandro's just a little longer than necessary as I handed him my number. He called two days later, and we decided to meet at Piazza Nazionale, just a couple of blocks from the pizzeria. I was wearing American jeans and a T-shirt that said, "The Cars," with a photo of a girl smiling behind a steering wheel. Sandro was also wearing jeans, but his T-shirt was plain white. I was mesmerized by his nipples and flat stomach. Clearly, his boss didn't let him take home much leftover pizza.

"Want to get some coffee?" I asked.

Sandro shook his head. "I'm too poor to do anything that fun," he said. "I even had to call you from a pay phone since I don't have a line myself. Do you mind just sitting for a bit?"

I shrugged, unsure if I wanted to admit my own poverty this early. At the same time, I didn't want him to think I felt he was beneath me. "Do you like working in the pizzeria?" I asked. "Any plans to do something else?"

It was his turn to shrug now. "I'm a zingaro," he said. "No birth certificate. No ID. I'll never be able to get a good job."

"A zingaro?" I repeated. "You look awfully pale for a gypsy." Almost no one used the term "Roma" in a country whose capital bore the same name.

"There was probably an American serviceman somewhere in my family tree." He grinned.

"Where are you from? Your accent's different."

"Up north," he replied, but his smile faded. "I don't want to talk about that."

I nodded. "My father works for *Il Mattino*," I said after a moment. "I've got a job in the newspaper's mailroom. You have to know someone to get even a low level position anywhere in this town. It's a start."

"Sounds a little stuffy," said Sandro, wrinkling his nose. "I just want to be free."

"It's easier to be free when you have money." I was thinking more about my own situation than his and didn't realize how my comment might sound until after I said it.

He shook his head. "I feel free every day of my life. Even with Cerasuolo breathing down my neck at work."

I took a deep breath and blurted out what I'd been thinking since the first moment I'd met him. "Do you feel free enough to spend the night with me?"

Sandro's face first registered surprise, but he followed that expression with a big smile. "Does tonight work for you?"

We walked to my apartment on Via Parma, Sandro explaining that he lived just a few blocks away on Vico Tutti Santi. I hoped he was hinting we could continue seeing each other easily. Scaffolding covered the building next to mine. Empty cardboard boxes and dog feces dotted the sidewalk.

Still, the neighborhood wasn't as grungy as the ghetto on the other side of Via Roma. I showed Sandro into my apartment. I couldn't give much of a tour, of course, as I only had the one bedroom, and a kitchen even smaller than my tiny bathroom. Sandro was trembling as I took his hand.

"What's wrong?" I asked.

"I-I've never done this before."

"But you sounded so smooth back in the piazza."

"Well, it's all about putting on a show, isn't it?" He smiled nervously. "I've *wanted* to do this for a long time. I've thought about it a lot. It's just a little scary now that it's happening." He paused for a moment. "Have you…?"

I nodded. I'd had sex with a cousin when I was fourteen and then later with a boy in my liceo. And then with a teacher in my liceo. But it was hard to do much while still living with my parents. That only gave me a few months in my own apartment without supervision, and I didn't have enough money to go to any clubs where I might meet men. Since I'd never done anything sexual as an adult, either, I was almost as nervous as Sandro.

I pulled off his T-shirt and he pulled off mine. We took our own shoes off, and while I wanted to be the one to pull his pants down, I let him finish disrobing on his own. We stood staring at each other by the foot of the bed.

"You're not a zingaro," I said, pointing. Sandro was circumcised. His brow furrowed at my statement and he started to protest. "You're a Jew," I concluded. "That's okay. I have nothing against Christ-killers."

Sandro's mouth fell open.

"Cretino." I laughed. "I'm kidding. As many hang-ups as Catholics have, I'm glad you're Jewish."

Sandro looked at the floor with a weary expression, and I vowed to learn more about Jews so that even my jokes wouldn't be so prejudiced. But I had something more pressing on my mind at the moment. I pulled Sandro close and hugged him loosely, rubbing my hairy chest softly against his bare chest. He closed his eyes and shuddered.

We climbed into bed together and began kissing. Knowing this was Sandro's first time, I made sure to go slow and make the event memorable. After such a long wait myself, I wanted to go slow for my own benefit as well. Two hours passed before we finished. "I feel like I should offer you a cigarette," I said, "but I don't smoke."

"I don't smoke, either. You have any music you can play?"

I slipped a cassette into my player, and soon Al Bano and Romina Power were singing "Felicità," low so as not to disturb the neighbors. "Kind of sappy, I know," I said, "but I've liked Romina Power ever since I learned her father was gay."

"Gay," Sandro repeated, looking at the ceiling. Then he turned to me. "Can I see you again sometime?"

I smiled and reached over to give him a kiss.

We began dating regularly, calling each other boyfriend right from the beginning. One afternoon we walked through Capodimonte park. Another afternoon we caught the funicolare up into the ghetto. On yet another occasion, we strolled around Piazza Carlo Terzo, memorable not because Sandro let his arm touch mine as we sat on a bench but because we witnessed a Camorra killing not five meters away.

We walked along the waterfront one evening in the rain. Sandro showed me the spot on Castel dell'Ovo where he worked his first job as a fisherman, a job he loathed but which gave him enough money to move from a rented room to his own apartment. Sandro's hours at the pizzeria were awful, so we couldn't see each other as often as I wished.

He slept over two nights a week, even if we didn't have much chance to do anything other than talk about pizza and office mail and then have sex. He invited me to his place once, but the one time was enough. The place was so damaged from the earthquake a couple of years before that

I was surprised it hadn't been condemned. We spent the rest of our nights together at my apartment.

"Maybe you *are* a gypsy," I said one evening after we'd been talking about movies for a while. "You know so little about Totò and Nino Manfredi and Claudia Cardinale. A Jew would be better educated."

He smiled but didn't answer.

We went to a neighborhood bar for some acqua Ferrarelle, a real luxury, and Sandro put a coin in the jukebox, singing "Sarà Perché Ti Amo" as he danced across the floor. He finished on his knees, taking my hand in his and giving it a kiss. I looked about nervously. Napoletani weren't the most progressive of people. A young woman drinking an aranciata hissed "Finocchi!" loudly and then walked up to us as if she might hit us.

"Valeria," she said, her hands on her hips. When her frown turned into a smile, we introduced ourselves as well. "My brother Gennaro's gay," she went on. "Dad beats him every time he stays out all night." She shrugged. "But what's a guy gonna do?" She lifted her hands upward in frustrated supplication. "Dad would absolutely murder me if I stayed out, and that's no exaggeration."

"What time do you have to be home?" I asked.

"10:00. Enough time to have a little fun, but not much. Gotta be heading back now."

"You two should come over to our place some night and dance," said Sandro. It was the first time he referred to my apartment as ours. I found I liked the sound of it. That night after we made love, I asked if he wanted to move in.

"We've only been dating six weeks," he said.

"Seven."

"Seven," he conceded.

"Do you love me?" I asked.

He smiled. "It's just that getting married so soon seems like something people in my family would do."

"Your gypsy family?" I asked. "Or your Jewish one?"

The following Sunday, Sandro moved the few clothes and other belongings he had into my apartment. Perhaps with our combined income, we could now eat out in a real restaurant once in a while or go see a movie. There were posters for a new Fellini film plastered all about the neighborhood next to the various death notices. I wanted to go with Sandro to Sorrento and Castellammare. I also wanted to take him to Capri to see how beautiful it was, though I wasn't sure anything was more beautiful than looking at him across the table from me in the kitchen first thing in the morning.

About a week after we officially became a couple, two Jehovah's Witnesses knocked on our door. Sandro came up to see who I was talking to and grew even paler than usual.

"Non ci interesse," he said curtly and shut the door. Later that night, he awoke from a nightmare, sitting bolt upright in the bed. "You okay?" I asked, taking his hand.

"Y-yes," he replied. "I am now."

"What does 'el dair' mean?" I asked. "You kept saying it in your sleep. Are you Spanish?" Maybe that accent he had wasn't even Italian.

"Non ne voglio parlare."

"But why, sweetie? Why don't you want to talk about it?"

"Non ne voglio parlare," he said again. He put his head back down on the pillow, and I let my arm drape across him as we both fell back to sleep.

We had Gennaro and Valeria over most Saturday nights for the next little while. Sandro could mimic any singer he wanted, entertaining us with "Una Notte Che Vola Via," "Una Sporca Poesia," "Romantici," and "Maledetta Primavera." How he could sound just like Loretta Goggi was beyond me.

One night, Gennaro asked if he could stay overnight with us. I kissed him on one cheek while Sandro kissed him on the other as we said no.

Things were getting worse at the pizzeria. Cerasuolo was yelling at Sandro more and more and once slapped him across the face. "You've got to find another job," I told him as we undressed that night, looking at the mark the man had left.

"I can't," Sandro replied. "I'm a gypsy. I don't have any papers. No one will hire me."

He started tapping the side of his head with the butt of one hand, groaning softly.

"I talked to my father. He knows someone who can get you a job as a door to door salesman."

"*No!*" Sandro squeezed his eyes shut and began swaying slightly side to side.

"Then get a job in a café," I said. "Get a job in a libreria."

"I'm a gypsy," he repeated. "I don't have any papers!"

He now began smacking the butt of his hand against his forehead, his eyes squeezed shut even more tightly. I wondered if he was having a seizure.

Or if maybe he was a little crazy.

I wondered if he loved me enough to tell me what was going on.

And if I loved him enough to listen.

"Stop it," I said. I caressed his upper arms until he slowly stopped moving. "Tell me the truth."

"I-I'm a gypsy."

I pulled him down onto the bed beside me and wrapped an arm around him.

"Sandro."

And then it came out. Sandro was really Kevin Stovall of Orem, Utah. He'd been a Mormon missionary here in Italy and had known before the end of his first month that he never wanted to go back to America. He studied the language longer each day than the time allotted and had a good ear to begin with, so by the time his two-year assignment was nearing an end, he could convince most people he was from "up north." Napoletani had such a sloppy accent to begin with that anyone speaking crisply seemed uppercrust.

"I couldn't go back to my family," he said, "once I knew I was gay and needed a man. They'd be so disappointed."

"What did you tell them?"

He shook his head. "I ran away in the middle of the night. I never told anyone anything."

"But Sandro—I mean, Kevin—they must be worried sick."

"Don't call me Kevin. My name is Sandro now."

"Sandro, you've *got* to call your parents."

He put his head in his hands. "What could I possibly say?"

"Even the truth is better than what they must be imagining."

"I'll think about it, Gaetano. Really, I will." He smiled. "You've already made my life better than it ever was before. Even getting slapped at work can't change that."

But I couldn't let the man I loved continue in that job. I understood now why Sandro didn't have any papers. He didn't want anyone to know he was American. Of course, even as an American, he wouldn't be able to work without a permit. But if he wanted to pass himself off as an Italian, that really did put him in the same position as the zingari. Unless…

I knew a guy at the newspaper who said he knew a guy in the Camorra. I arranged to meet the man and ask to have a birth certificate and ID made. I expected it would cost enough that I'd have to talk my father into a small loan, but the guy with the Camorra agreed I could pay simply by transporting something for him. He didn't say what it was and I didn't ask. But a week later, someone showed up at my apartment with a camera, and a few days after that, Sandro had his papers.

"Jobs still aren't easy to find around here," I said, "but at least now you have a fighting chance."

"I would take any job in the world as long as I could come home to you every evening."

"Now you're sounding like Romina Power."

"Or at least like her father."

Three more months passed. Sandro did call his family and tell them about us. Instead of being relieved to hear he was okay, they hung up the phone and made no effort to contact him again. Maybe someday they'd change their minds.

My father was unhappy about my living arrangements, too, but said that as long as I didn't tell anyone at the newspaper, he wouldn't disown me. When my mother invited Sandro over for dinner, I knew we'd passed our biggest hurdle. Sandro entertained everyone with an a capella rendition of "Storie di Tutti i Giorni" that left even my father impressed.

"You know," he told me over the phone the following day, "your…friend…has a strong presence in front of people. He'd make a good tour guide. I know someone who runs a tour company in Pompeii—he did some advertising with the paper—and I think I can get him to talk to Sandro. If you want."

"We want."

I didn't tell Sandro until the appointment was confirmed. "Make sure he knows you can give tours in both English and Italian," I said. Sandro had to call in sick in order to meet with the owner of the tour company, which left Cerasuolo yelling and making threats, but Gennaro filled in for the day and eventually took over the position when Sandro got the new job.

We promised to help Gennaro find something better, too.

A month later, once we'd finally saved a little money, Sandro and I held a party at our place to celebrate a new beginning. Gennaro came with Vittorio, a guy he'd just met over the counter at the pizzeria, and Valeria came with Stefano, a guy she'd met over an aranciata a couple of weeks earlier, who was cuter than any of the rest of us. Sandro sang "L'italiano" quite convincingly but saved his last performance until after the others had left. "Tu Cosa Fai Stasera?" he asked.

And I answered by holding out my hand.

Chapter One from *The Camper Killings*

Blood was dripping from Nick's camper door. I'd promised to bring the man some groceries on my way home from work, but he couldn't be so starved yet he'd passed out and hit his head. No mouse or even rat trap would create that kind of blood spill. And Nick would hardly have caught one of the neighborhood coyotes and slaughtered it for food, no matter how desperate life could be for someone unhoused.

He'd eaten roadkill raccoon once but swore he'd never do it again.

The blood was only a trickle, and I tried to convince myself Nick had taken up painting with acrylics to while away the hours. Perhaps he'd finally braved his first sip of red wine and gotten so drunk he dropped the bottle. Maybe this was evidence of a bladder infection. A kidney stone. I knocked on the door.

"Nick?" I called out. "You okay? Nick?"

No sound other than the swoosh of a bicycle zooming downhill on the other side of the street. No movement inside the camper.

I repeated the mantra I made myself say out loud at least twice a day. "If you are brave, you are likely to make mistakes. Be brave anyway."

I set my two bags of groceries on the sidewalk and pushed down on the handle. The latch clicked. "Nick?"

I pulled the door open and peered cautiously inside. Nick was sitting on the camper's tiny loveseat, leaning against a narrow closet. An open plastic wrapper on a tiny pull-down table revealed the last two slices of wheat and walnut bread from a loaf I'd bought him the week before. Underneath the table was a black garbage bag filled with trash that I was scheduled to take away today after dropping off Nick's groceries.

I staggered and caught myself on the doorframe, remembering the death oaths I'd made in the Idaho Falls temple years before. We'd all promised upon pain of death never to divulge the secret handshakes needed to get us into heaven. Those of us taking out our endowments agreed to be disemboweled if we revealed the secret. We agreed to have our throats slit.

Nick Degraff had been Mormon.

His throat was slit.

I closed my eyes and swallowed the bile in my mouth. Then I pulled out my cell and dialed 9-1-1.

***

Detective Stalder surveyed me again with a quick flicker of his eyes. He'd done it several times already as we talked outside the camper. "Morgan sounds like a girl's name," he said. It was the third homophobic thing he'd said since he and his partner had arrived.

I thought about Inspector Vivaldi and shrugged. "Stalder sounds like a prick's name." When the detective scowled, I added casually, "So it's plenty butch, I suppose."

Detective Stalder looked unsure if he'd been insulted or not. But if he was too dense to understand, that was on him. He turned to his partner, Detective Klimczyk. "Seems Mr. Degraff brought the wrong guy home for sex."

Detective Klimczyk looked on impassively.

"Nick wasn't gay," I said. The detective was making assumptions about Nick based on my own appearance and manner, as if gay and straight men could never be friends. And did he not think women capable of murder? Didn't he watch *Law and Order*?

Detective Stalder looked me up and down yet again. "Uh huh."

"You seem to have exceptionally strong gaydar for a straight man," I said in as neutral a tone as I could muster. It was difficult not to hear disdain in his voice, even if intellectually I realized I might be imagining it. Years ago, one of my fuck buddies had been stabbed to death by a gay basher, and the responding officers had basically determined Kevin got what he deserved. Before I came out, I remembered my bishop announcing the excommunication of a young man in the Elders Quorum. "He's dying of AIDS," Bishop Hauer had added. "Let's all pray he repents while he has time. But if he chooses spiritual death the way he chose physical death, so be it."

"Listen, you—"

"You already told us Mr. Degraff was getting a messy divorce," Detective Klimczyk interrupted. "How do you know he wasn't gay? People have secrets." He raised an eyebrow. "No offense, Mr. Beylerian, but just because he wasn't interested in *you* doesn't mean he wasn't gay."

Both detectives were about forty, white, and in good enough shape that I'd have happily knelt for them under other circumstances, but obnoxiousness was a real turn off for pretty much any body type.

To be fair, it was mostly Stalder who was obnoxious, though it was difficult to see the other detective as his own person since they worked as a team. Klimczyk did have sexy ears, though, so I wanted to give him the benefit of the doubt.

The kind of ears you wanted to slowly caress with your tongue and...

"*You* could probably turn a gay man straight." Detective Stalder smirked, pointing a stubby finger at my belly.

"Are these the investigative techniques they're teaching these days?" I shot back. "I might be fat, but I'm good. Nick had me give him blow jobs all the time. He had no reason to lie about his orientation."

"I'll pass," Stalder said.

"I wasn't offering."

"Mr. Beylerian," Klimczyk interjected softly, "we'll investigate every possibility, including whether or not this was a sex crime."

The truth was I had no idea if Nick's murder was sex-related or not. I couldn't think of any reason at all someone would want to kill him. I *liked* the guy. We played backgammon together. We chatted while playing gin rummy. If I hadn't liked him, there were plenty of other homeless folks I could have helped instead. There was certainly no shortage.

Nick still resisted granting a temple divorce to Amanda despite having already agreed to a civil one, but it was hard to imagine she'd have killed him over it. Or hired someone else to do it. Nick and I joked that instead of being a Stepford Wife, Amanda was a Schroedinger's Wife, married and not married to him at the same time. But then Nick's smile would fade and he'd say, "As long as our marriage survives on any plane, there's still hope it's not dead."

"Did you ever see him with anyone else?" Klimczyk asked.

I shrugged. "I probably only spent two or three hours a week with him," I said. "That leaves…what?…a hundred and sixty-something hours I can't claim to have witnessed."

But it wasn't as if anyone was fighting him over his parking spot alongside Takahashi Gardens. There was nothing besides trees and bushes along this stretch of Renton Avenue. And it was far enough uphill that no one casually walked by who wasn't headed this way with a firm destination in mind.

It wasn't Rainier and Henderson, where I'd once dodged bullets from a drive-by shooting, or where I'd witnessed two teenage girls mug an old man about my age.

Another day at that same intersection, I'd seen a patrol car in the bank's parking lot, two officers watching as a young black woman in flashy hooker clothes waited on the corner. Two black men in a faded gray pickup truck pulled into the lot and honked. The young woman had walked over and climbed in between them. The patrol car didn't move as the truck drove off.

Part of me had been glad the officers didn't harass the woman. But another part of me had worried, wondering if she would make it home safely.

"Think he was paying runaways?" Stalder asked. "Street hustlers?"

"Insecure straight men leading a murder investigation," I said. This wasn't Capitol Hill, after all, or Pioneer Square. "You guys think about dick even more than gay men do."

Stalder took a half step forward. Klimczyk put a hand on his arm.

"Me thinketh the detective doth obsess too much," I said.

I didn't even know why I was antagonizing them. It was only going to make life harder for all of us. And it wasn't going to help Nick any.

He needed help, even if he was dead.

Nick's ex had been turning their kids against him. It was almost all we talked about, strategies for winning back their love despite the lies Amanda was telling them.

I was the only other person besides Amanda he'd ever had sex with. And he had been the one to proposition me. He needed some way to deal with both his stress and anger, and he said that if he limited his "release" to a single person he wasn't attracted to, he could convince himself he was only transgressing and not sinning.

A Mormon distinction.

In addition to grocery shopping, sex was one of the few other volunteer activities I participated in. A firefighter here. A police officer there. A straight neighbor whose wife with dementia had been moved into an assisted living facility. And a couple of homeless men.

Lots of folks had limited options but everyone deserved at least the opportunity for sex. It was a principle I believed in as strongly as mail-in voting. As a result, apparently, I gave off "whatever you need, dude" vibes. God only knew how. I embarrassed myself every time I looked in a mirror. So it was almost always other guys doing the asking. Most of the men didn't even seem gay. I assumed it was impolite to ask, the way prisoners never asked each other why they were doing time. Now that I was in the bariatric program and losing weight in preparation for surgery, guys had stopped asking only for blow jobs. Some now wanted to fuck me, too.

It was hardly a sacrifice on my part. I had plenty of my own frustration and anger to deal with. I could often hear Tony beating off in the bathroom right before bed, loud on purpose to warn me not to get frisky later.

Last week, just as I heard him approaching climax, I broke into the chorus of "Suddenly Seymour" right outside the bathroom door.

"Doesn't matter," Stalder said, shrugging. "If he let you into his camper, he could have—"

"He was afraid," I said.

"Of?" asked Klimczyk.

"Everyone."

A few weeks back, a Filipino teenager had been shot several blocks over while opening his front door. A month earlier, a white high school football player had been shot in his car in front of his house. And a retired black nun had been murdered in her home a year ago by a homeless man she volunteered with.

"Except you?" Stalder said with a smile. "You realize you're making yourself the most likely suspect."

I shook my head. "I'm an ex-Mormon," I said. "I'd never be a Danite."

"What the fuck—"

"Look it up."

***

Before walking the last few blocks home, I handed the two bags of groceries to Elijah, Nick's closest homeless neighbor. I suppose homeless wasn't the best word. Unhoused, either. Several folks along this stretch of Renton Avenue lived in campers, vans, RVs, and long-haul trucker cabs. They all technically had roofs over their heads, just extremely inadequate ones.

I was too lazy and self-centered to do any real advocacy work, but I did try to pick up trash bags from several of the homeless folks along Renton. Made me feel more useful than I really was, and it did reduce illegal dumping in the gully beside Takahashi Gardens.

Mr. Takahashi had run a nursery in Rainier Beach early in the twentieth century. He and his family had been interned in a concentration camp during WWII, but after the war, he still ended up donating his property to the City of Seattle, and they eventually turned it into a Japanese garden.

"Morgan," Tony said as I walked in the door, "what took you so long? Dinner's been ready for ages."

"Sorry, sweetie." I kissed my husband and then wrapped my arms around him and didn't let go.

"Is something wrong?" Tony asked. "What happened?"

"Nick was murdered in his camper."

"Jesus, Morgan, you need to stop hanging out with dangerous people."

I took a step back. "You used to take out the nun's trash, didn't you?"

"That was different. *She* wasn't dangerous."

"Elijah doesn't seem dangerous. I'll start visiting him now."

"Jesus, Morgan."

Nick had given me a silver Morgan dollar last week, said it had been given to him by his grandfather, who'd claimed that *his* father had received it from Lorenzo Snow.

People sometimes gave away their prized possessions before taking their own lives.

Had Nick *asked* someone to kill him? Provoked someone?

"I'm going to wash my face."

"Hope you're in the mood for chili."

I nodded and continued to the bathroom. The sad truth was that I was in fact hungry. I was always hungry. Drinking lots of water didn't help. Using little spoons and forks didn't help. Keeping a food diary didn't help.

It simply added to the mortification.

I didn't blame Tony for not understanding that beans had too many carbs for me. It seemed unfair for the bariatric clinic to force me to lose twenty pounds on my own as one of a dozen hoops I had to jump through to qualify for surgery. If I could lose that much weight by myself, I wouldn't need to cut two-thirds of my stomach off.

Still, unexpected gum surgery in early August had forced me onto a liquid diet for a week, during which I'd lost an amazing fifteen pounds, so I'd kept it up for an additional week and lost six more. I'd gone from 244 pounds—the lowest weight at which I qualified for the program—down to 219. But it was a constant battle not to regain even a pound. If I did, I could still get kicked out of the program.

Tony had weighed 160 when we first met seventeen years ago. He weighed 164 now.

"You don't like it?" Tony asked after I joined him at the table without picking up my spoon. He frowned. "I tried not to make it too spicy."

"I'm sure it's great," I said. "I'm just not very hungry after seeing Nick with his throat slit." He'd interpret any other explanation as a personal attack.

"Jesus, Morgan. I'm eating."

I shrugged. "I need to take advantage of every inspiration not to eat."

Tony rolled his eyes. "Fine. Keep hanging out with dangerous people. Maybe you'll be shot in the stomach and the doctor will be forced to do the bypass sooner."

He wasn't really being mean, I kept telling myself. Not intentionally, anyway. He just had an odd sense of humor that seemed to tickle his own funny bone more than anyone else's.

"How much money do you think a homeless man keeps in his camper?" I asked.

"Huh?"

"Why do you suppose he was killed?"

Tony shook his head, clearly unhappy with the topic. "Maybe it was just someone killing random homeless people. Like that serial killer in Stockton. Or the guy who set that homeless man on fire in Chicago. These things happen all the time." He shrugged.

I took another sip of seltzer water. Lime was my favorite, and Tony always remembered to buy it. Technically, I wasn't supposed to drink anything carbonated once I was in the bariatric program because it irritated the stomach lining. But I needed something with "body." I was sure I could stop before having my endoscopy and again when it came time for the actual surgery. There weren't any twelve-step programs for seltzer water, after all.

I was already able to stand up from the sofa now using only my legs, without needing to push up with my arms at the same time.

The liquid diet had forced me to take in only 20 to 30 grams of carbs a day. I'd been able to eliminate insulin injections completely for six weeks. Once I was back on solid food, though, even trying to keep my carbs low, I couldn't keep them low enough. I'd eventually had to start injecting again once a day, and within another two weeks was injecting twice a day as I'd been doing for years.

One of the side effects of insulin was weight gain.

It was also one of the side effects of my HIV meds.

"A pedestrian was killed in a hit-and-run on Capitol Hill," Tony said, taking advantage of my silence to shift the conversation.

"Anyone we know?"

He shook his head.

"That's three pedestrians hit by cars in the past two weeks," I noted. All hit-and-run. Was this the work of a serial killer, too?

"And a home invasion in Ballard."

I picked some cheese off the top of my chili and ate it. "I suppose it's still a home invasion if your home is a camper, isn't it?"

And it would still be a home invasion if someone broke into your tent. Or accosted you in your sleeping bag.

Tony put his spoon down. "You're killing me with all this homeless talk." He stuck a finger in his chili and pulled it out, orange now from the sauce and spices. He rubbed it on the ridges of his left ear.

I stood up and moved to the other side of the table, leaning down and licking every drop of chili sauce off him.

"You don't like the beans," he said, "but you'll still eat a full protein, right?" He swung his legs away from the table, unzipped, and closed his eyes.

I was up for almost anything that kept me away from the fridge.

What Readers Have Said

Townsend's stories are "a gay *Portnoy's Complaint* of Mormonism. Salacious, sweet, sad, insightful, insulting, religiously ethnic, quirky-faithful, and funny."

D. Michael Quinn, author of *The Mormon Hierarchy: Origins of Power*

"Told from a believably conversational first-person perspective, [*The Abominable Gayman*'s] novelistic focus on Anderson's journey to thoughtful self-acceptance allows for greater character development than often seen in short stories, which makes this well-paced work rich and satisfying, and one of Townsend's strongest. An extremely important contribution to the field of Mormon fiction." Named to Kirkus Reviews' Best of 2011.

Kirkus Reviews

"The thirteen stories in *Mormon Underwear* capture this struggle [between Mormonism and homosexuality] with humor, sadness, insight, and sometimes shocking details....*Mormon Underwear* provides compelling stories, literally from the inside-out."

Niki D'Andrea, *Phoenix New Times*

"Townsend's lively writing style and engaging characters [in *Zombies for Jesus*] make for stories which force us to wake up, smell the (prohibited) coffee, and review our attitudes with regard to reading dogma so doggedly. These are tales which revel in the individual tics and quirks which make us human, Mormon or not, gay or not…"

A.J. Kirby, *The Short Review*

"The Rift," from *The Abominable Gayman*, is a "fascinating tale of an untenable situation…a *tour de force*."

David Lenson, editor, *The Massachusetts Review*

"Pronouncing the Apostrophe," from *The Golem of Rabbi Loew*, is "quiet and revealing, an intriguing tale…"

Sima Rabinowitz, Literary Magazine Review, *NewPages.com*

The Circumcision of God is "a collection of short stories that consider the imperfect, silenced majority of Mormons, who may in fact be [the Church's] best hope….[The book leaves] readers regretting the church's willingness to marginalize those who best exemplify its ideals: those who love fiercely despite all obstacles, who brave challenges at great personal risk and who always choose the hard, higher road."

Kirkus Reviews

In *Mormon Fairy Tales*, Johnny Townsend displays "both a wicked sense of irony and a deep well of compassion."

Kel Munger, *Sacramento News and Review*

Zombies for Jesus is "eerie, erotic, and magical."

Publishers Weekly

"While [Townsend's] many touching vignettes draw deeply from Mormon mythology, history, spirituality and culture, [*Mormon Fairy Tales*] is neither a gaudy act of proselytism nor angry protest literature from an ex-believer. Like all good fiction, his stories are simply about the joys, the hopes and the sorrows of people."

Kirkus Reviews

"In *Let the Faggots Burn* author Johnny Townsend restores this tragic event [the UpStairs Lounge fire] to its proper place in LGBT history and reminds us that the victims of the blaze were not just 'statistics,' but real people with real lives, families, and friends."

Jesse Monteagudo, *The Bilerico Project*

In *Let the Faggots Burn*, "Townsend's heart-rending descriptions of the victims…seem to [make them] come alive once more."

Kit Van Cleave, *OutSmart Magazine*

Marginal Mormons is "an irreverent, honest look at life outside the mainstream Mormon Church….Throughout his musings on sin and forgiveness, Townsend beautifully demonstrates his characters' internal, perhaps irreconcilable struggles….Rather than anger and disdain, he offers an honest portrayal of people searching for meaning and community in their lives, regardless of their life choices or secrets." Named to Kirkus Reviews' Best of 2012.

Kirkus Reviews

The stories in *The Mormon Victorian Society* "register the new openness and confidence of gay life in the age of same-sex marriage….What hasn't changed is Townsend's wry, conversational prose, his subtle evocations of character and social dynamics, and his deadpan humor. His warm empathy still glows in this intimate yet clear-eyed engagement with Mormon theology and folkways. Funny, shrewd and finely wrought dissections of the awkward contradictions—and surprising harmonies—between conscience and desire." Named to Kirkus Reviews' Best of 2013.

Kirkus Reviews

"This collection of short stories [*The Mormon Victorian Society*] featuring gay Mormon characters slammed [me] in the face from the first page, wrestled my heart and mind to the floor, and left me panting and wanting more by the end. Johnny Townsend has created so many memorable characters in such few pages. I went weeks thinking about this book. It truly touched me."

Tom Webb, *A Bear on Books*

Dragons of the Book of Mormon is an "entertaining collection....Townsend's prose is sharp, clear, and easy to read, and his characters are well rendered..."

Publishers Weekly

"The pre-eminent documenter of alternative Mormon lifestyles...Townsend has a deep understanding of his characters, and his limpid prose, dry humor and well-grounded (occasionally magical) realism make their spiritual conundrums both compelling and entertaining. [*Dragons of the Book of Mormon* is] [a]nother of Townsend's critical but affectionate and absorbing tours of Mormon discontent." Named to Kirkus Reviews' Best of 2014.

Kirkus Reviews

In *Gayrabian Nights*, "Townsend's prose is always limpid and evocative, and…he finds real drama and emotional depth in the most ordinary of lives."

Kirkus Reviews

Gayrabian Nights is a "complex revelation of how seriously soul damaging the denial of the true self can be."

Ryan Rhodes, author of *Free Electricity*

Gayrabian Nights "was easily the most original book I've read all year. Funny, touching, topical, and thoroughly enjoyable."

Rainbow Awards

Lying for the Lord is "one of the most gripping books that I've picked up for quite a while. I love the author's writing style, alternately cynical, humorous, biting, scathing, poignant, and touching…. This is the third book of his that I've read, and all are equally engaging. These are stories that need to be told, and the author does it in just the right way."

Heidi Alsop, *Ex-Mormon Foundation Board Member*

In *Lying for the Lord*, Townsend "gets under the skin of his characters to reveal their complexity and conflicts….shrewd, evocative [and] wryly humorous."

Kirkus Reviews

In *Missionaries Make the Best Companions*, "the author treats the clash between religious dogma and liberal humanism with vivid realism, sly humor, and subtle feeling as his characters try to figure out their true missions in life. Another of Townsend's rich dissections of Mormon failures and uncertainties…" Named to Kirkus Reviews' Best of 2015.

Kirkus Reviews

In *Invasion of the Spirit Snatchers*, "Townsend, a confident and practiced storyteller, skewers the hypocrisies and eccentricities of his characters with precision and affection. The outlandish framing narrative is the most consistent source of shock and humor, but the stories do much to ground the reader in the world—or former world—of the characters….A funny, charming tale about a group of Mormons facing the end of the world."

Kirkus Reviews

"Townsend's collection [*The Washing of Brains*] once again displays his limpid, naturalistic prose, skillful narrative chops, and his subtle insights into psychology…Well-crafted dispatches on the clash between religion and self-fulfillment…"

Kirkus Reviews

"While the author is generally at his best when working as a satirist, there are some fine, understated touches in these tales [*The Last Days Linger*] that will likely affect readers in subtle ways....readers should come away impressed by the deep empathy he shows for all his characters—even the homophobic ones."

Kirkus Reviews

"Written in a conversational style that often uses stories and personal anecdotes to reveal larger truths, this immensely approachable book [*Racism by Proxy*] skillfully serves its intended audience of White readers grappling with complex questions regarding race, history, and identity. The author's frequent references to the Church of Jesus Christ of Latter-day Saints may be too niche for readers unfamiliar with its idiosyncrasies, but Townsend generally strikes a perfect balance of humor, introspection, and reasoned arguments that will engage even skeptical readers."

Kirkus Reviews

Orgy at the STD Clinic portrays "an all-too real scenario that Townsend skewers to wincingly accurate proportions...[with] instant classic moments courtesy of his punchy, sassy, sexy lead character..."

Jim Piechota, *Bay Area Reporter*

Orgy at the STD Clinic is "…a triumph of humane sensibility. A richly textured saga that brilliantly captures the fraying social fabric of contemporary life."

Kirkus Reviews